Coming here had been a terrible mistake.

If she could have clawed her way out, she would have fled the dream. But it continued to hold her fast.

The door opened to reveal a man dressed all in black, and in place of a face, he had a death mask.

"You," he whispered. "How did you get here?"

Her only answer was a scream. She would have run, but her feet were rooted to the floor. And the figure was coming toward her.

Far away, she heard someone calling her name. It was Mack.

"Jamie, wake up. Come back to me."

She wanted to. She wanted to get out of this awful place. She wanted to come back to him.

She felt his hand clamp around hers. Sensed his desperation. She could hear him. Touch him. But she couldn't see him. All she could see was the man in black advancing on her step by step.

USA TODAY BESTSELLING AUTHOR

REBECCA YORK

RUTH GLICK WRITING AS REBECCA YORK

SOLID AS STEELE

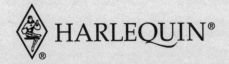

HARLEQUIN®

TORONTO • NEW YORK • LONDON
AMSTERDAM • PARIS • SYDNEY • HAMBURG
STOCKHOLM • ATHENS • TOKYO • MILAN • MADRID
PRAGUE • WARSAW • BUDAPEST • AUCKLAND

Recycling programs
for this product may
not exist in your area.

ISBN-13: 978-0-373-69523-2

SOLID AS STEELE

Copyright © 2011 by Ruth Glick

ABOUT THE AUTHOR

Award-winning, bestselling novelist Ruth Glick, who writes as Rebecca York, is the author of more than one hundred books, including her popular 43 Light Street series for Harlequin Intrigue. Ruth says she has the best job in the world. Not only does she get paid for telling stories, she's also the author of twelve cookbooks. Ruth and her husband, Norman, travel frequently, researching locales for her novels and searching out new dishes for her cookbooks.

Books by Rebecca York

HARLEQUIN INTRIGUE
706—PHANTOM LOVER*
717—INTIMATE STRANGERS*
745—BOYS IN BLUE
      "Jordan"
765—OUT OF NOWHERE*
783—UNDERCOVER ENCOUNTER
828—SPELLBOUND
885—RILEY'S RETRIBUTION
912—THE SECRET NIGHT*
946—CHAIN REACTION
994—ROYAL LOCKDOWN
1017—RETURN OF THE WARRIOR*
1072—SOLDIER CAGED*
1089—CHRISTMAS SPIRIT
1150—MORE THAN A MAN*
1187—POWERHOUSE
1215—GUARDING GRACE*
1256—SOLID AS STEELE*

*43 Light Street

CAST OF CHARACTERS

Jamie Shepherd—She'd had nightmares for years, but she'd thought they were over.

Craig Shepherd—He'd been the love of Jamie's life; but after he died, could she put her life back together?

Mack Steele—Would the detective keep his objectivity when Jamie dragged him into a murder investigation?

Gloria Wheeler—Did Jamie's mother wish her daughter well or ill?

Lynn Vaughn—Was she reaching out to Jamie?

Fred Hyde—Why was he punishing the residents of Gaptown?

Clark Landon—How far would Gloria's boyfriend go to get Jamie to leave town?

Tim Conrad—Did his murder fit into Jamie and Mack's fun-house investigation?

Jeanette Baker—She was another piece of the fun-house puzzle.

Chapter One

Jamie Shepherd struggled to claw her way back to consciousness, but the nightmare held her fast. She was in a dark, spooky funhouse, trying to find the exit to freedom.

Music from a slasher movie blared from hidden speakers. Eerie green light shimmered around her. And the air was thick with a horrible graveyard smell.

Coughing, pressing her hand over her mouth, she fought to escape, even when she knew on some instinctive level that it wasn't her dream. She clung to that secret knowledge as she ran down an endless hallway, her breath coming in great gasps, her terror increasing with every step.

Ahead of her was a blank wall. *Oh Lord!*

She was trapped.

Or maybe not. Struggling to control her fear, she began to slide her hands over the flat surface, searching for a seam or a latch, something that would let her escape from the monster that she knew was behind her.

Finally, her fingers found a small indentation. When she pressed into it, a door sprang outward so fast that she lost her footing and tumbled through.

As she scrambled to right herself, she found she was on a slide that carried her down into the darkness, then dumped her onto a cold cement floor.

She lay there panting, her shoulder throbbing where it had struck the floor. From far away she heard a train whistle blow. Then, much closer, a sound behind her froze the blood in her veins.

He was coming! She had to get away.

After dragging herself up, she stood in the darkness, trying not to let her breathing give her away.

From a speaker in the wall, a grating voice boomed, "You can't stay there."

"No more. Please. Let me go," she cried out.

"Not yet."

"What have I done to you?"

"You know."

"I don't! Please just let me out of here. I don't even know who you are."

"Of course you know."

"No!"

"I'll let you out if you can find the door. Go back upstairs."

As he spoke, a spotlight switched on, and she saw steps leading upward.

She clambered up, grasping the railing. At the top, she found herself in another corridor, this one lined with mirrors that distorted her image as they reflected her face and body.

Someone had spattered red paint on the floor. Or was it blood?

She looked behind her and saw a shadowed figure climbing the steps, his pace slow and deliberate, like he had all the time in the world.

A cry rose in her throat when she saw how he was dressed. He wore a black robe, and his face was a skull mask with glowing red eyes. She had seen him before. First just a glimpse. Then a fuller look. And some deep, primal instinct told her she was dead if he caught up with her.

"No! Please."

She couldn't let him get her. That thought filled every corner of her mind as she came to a place where the corridor divided.

Which way? Oh God, which way?

As he bore relentlessly down on her, she whimpered and chose the left-hand hallway. Only a few steps later, a bright light flashed in her eyes, almost blinding her, but she kept running because that was her only option.

Then out of the brightness, a black shape loomed in front of her.

It was *him*. Somehow he had circled around. He must have used a hidden passage, because now he was blocking her path. In his hand, she saw the glint of metal—the blade of a long, cruel knife.

She screamed and raised her arm, trying to defend herself. But the knife slashed into her flesh. As he pulled back and swung down for another blow, pain jolted through her.

Then mercifully, everything went black.

On a sob, Jamie woke, her fingers clawing at the sheet as she tried to drag herself out of the nightmare house and back to her own reality. To her own bed.

It had been a dream. Only a dream. But not about *her*. It was another woman desperately trying to escape from a madman and just as desperately reaching out to Jamie.

Now the contact had snapped off, vanished as if it had never existed. She wanted to deny that it had been real. Yet in the secret part of her mind, she couldn't convince herself that it was only a nightmare.

"No," she whispered, wrapping her arms around her shoulders and rocking back and forth as she willed it not to be true, but denial was not an option. She had been in that other woman's mind. Felt the terror coming off of her in waves. And Jamie was pretty sure that the scene of horror had taken place in Gaptown, Maryland, the small city in the state's western mountains where she had grown up.

She'd made what she considered her escape, and she'd vowed never to return to a place where she'd hated her life. Yet a woman from home had reached out to her and pulled her back.

That the contact was in her mind didn't make it any less real or any less terrifying, and it didn't absolve her of responsibility to do something.

She lay in bed shivering, her heart pounding like a drum inside her chest as she watched the headlights of cars travel across the ceiling and wondered whether one of the vehicles was coming for *her*.

"Stop it," she muttered. "You're safe in your own bed. That man isn't in Baltimore. He can't get you."

Yes. She was safe. But the other woman…

She pushed herself up and turned on the bedside lamp, looking around the familiar bedroom. The lamp's glow was enough for her to see the outlines of the sleek modern chest of drawers and the lower dresser that she'd selected because they were so different from the ugly orange maple pieces back home.

After slipping out of bed, she pressed her feet against the oak floorboards, shivering a little in the early-morning cold, then stood up, stiffening her knees to steady herself. Hugging her arms around her shoulders, she crossed to the bathroom, where she filled a glass and gulped down several swallows of water.

She set down the glass with a thunk, then leaned forward and peered at herself in the mirror, seeing her straight blond hair, her troubled blue eyes, the slight tilt of her nose, and lips that were chapped because of her bad habit of taking them between her teeth.

It was her face. Totally familiar. Yet in the dream she'd been someone else.

Someone she knew? Maybe. But she didn't want to deal with that now, because it made the nightmare all the more terrible.

She'd felt the woman's panic. Her terrible need to escape. And then the blackness at the end.

"Oh Lord," she murmured, her hands gripping the cold porcelain of the sink as she struggled with her confused thoughts. One thing she knew for sure. She didn't want to be alone.

She had to call someone.

She knew that her friend Jo O'Malley would listen to her and tell her what to do, even at two in the morning.

Back in the bedroom, she sat down and picked up the phone, calling the familiar number.

After two rings, a man's deep voice said, "Light Street Detective Agency."

When she didn't say anything, he asked, "Is anybody there?"

"I…I'm sorry," Jamie stammered. It wasn't Jo. Lord, why had she even thought that Jo would be in the office to answer the phone? She was home with her husband, Cam Randolph, and her children, Leo and Anna.

"Jamie?" the man on the other end of the line asked, and she was afraid she knew who he was.

"Mack?"

"Yes."

Her fingers gripped the receiver more tightly. Mack Steele was the last person she'd wanted to talk to, yet it turned out he was the one on duty.

"What's wrong?" he asked.

"I…nothing," she answered, feeling her heart start to pound all over again. There was plenty wrong, but she didn't want to talk about it with him. Not when she was in such a vulnerable state.

"It's something or you wouldn't have called. Is someone outside the house? Did they try to break in?"

She swallowed hard. "No. Nothing like that. I made a mistake," she said.

"Talk to me."

"I've got to go."

Before she could dig herself in any deeper, she replaced the receiver, then sat, shivering, on the side of the bed.

Jo would be in tomorrow. She'd go to her office before she reported to work at the 43 Light Street Lobby Shop, where she'd been a part-time clerk since she moved to Baltimore. They'd talk tomorrow.

She longed to crawl back into the warmth of the covers and lose herself in sleep again, but lying there would be a waste of time. She'd only end up staring at more car lights traveling across the ceiling and thinking about the woman. Or thinking about herself.

And the one rule she'd made after her husband, Craig, had been killed was that she wasn't going to lie in bed if there was no hope of going back to sleep. Better to get up and do something constructive.

Which was what?

She'd been working on some "baking in a jar" projects for the Lobby Shop. Each clear glass container had layers of dry ingredients like flour, spices and dried fruit that made a pretty pattern. But they were also practical—add some liquids and the ingredients made delicious baked goods. And she'd printed up easy directions for each one.

The jars had sold well during the holidays, and the shop owner, Sabrina Cassidy, had asked for more.

Jamie could put a few together tonight and take them to work with her in the morning.

Glad to have a sense of purpose, she padded to the closet and pulled out a pair of jeans and one of Craig's old plaid shirts that she liked to wear around the house. In the bathroom, she turned on the shower, hoping that hot water might wash away the chill from her skin.

IN THE OFFICE of the Light Street Detective Agency, Mack Steele turned toward the window, looking out over the sleeping city.

Jamie Shepherd had called a while ago, and he'd known from her voice that something was wrong. Then she'd hung up.

Probably because she didn't want to talk to *him*. Well, too bad. Something had spooked her, and he wasn't going to leave her alone and in trouble.

Trouble?

He clenched and unclenched his fists. Yeah, it had sounded like trouble. She was obviously worried about *something*. And she was all alone. Had been since Craig Shepherd had gotten killed in a hit and run accident last year.

Before he could change his mind he called Hunter Kelley.

"Yeah?" the sleepy voice asked.

"Sorry to bother you, but I have to go out, and I'm having calls transferred to your phone."

"There's a problem?"

"Maybe. Nothing I can't handle on my own." He didn't want to go into a long explanation, so he ended the call, strode out of the office and took the elevator to the basement, where he crossed the alley to the parking garage next door.

After climbing into his car, he turned right, heading for the quiet street in Ellicott City where Jamie lived.

She probably wouldn't want to see him at three in the morning, but she'd called the office, and she must have had a reason.

He couldn't think about Jamie without a familiar mixture of desire and guilt.

Her husband, Craig, had been his friend, one of his colleagues at the Light Street Detective Agency. The moment Mack had laid eyes on Craig's new girlfriend, Jamie Wheeler, he'd wished to hell he'd met her first. Because he wasn't going to cut in on a good guy like Craig, he'd kept his relationship with Jamie polite and distant, before she'd married his friend and after. Yet he'd had the feeling that she knew there was more to his interest in her than a bit of superficial conversation at office parties.

He'd kept an eye on Jamie. Just watching her with Craig, he'd known the marriage was good. The two of them were perfect for each other. And Craig had told Mack how happy he was. They'd bought a house, talked about kids, lived in the present and made plans for the future.

It had all blown up in Jamie's face ten months ago when Craig had gotten hit by a car that sped away, leaving her a widow. All of the Light Street men and women had rallied around Jamie, making it clear that she was still part of their extended family, and they were there for her.

He'd told himself it would be all right to let her know he was interested in being more than just friends. Only he'd never been able to do it because he couldn't let go of the notion that Craig should still be around. Not that he'd caused his friend's death, of course. Or even wished that Craig would disappear from the picture. But there was no denying the awkwardness between himself and Jamie. Whether it was because she was attracted to him and couldn't admit it or because he didn't know how to reveal his feelings for her, neither one of them had bridged the gap between them.

WHEN THE PHONE RANG, Jamie jumped. Who could that be at this time of night, she wondered.

Anticipating more trouble, she wiped her hands on a dish towel and picked up the receiver.

"Hello?"

"It's Mack. I'm outside. I didn't want to startle you by ringing the doorbell."

She glanced at the clock on the stove, then swallowed hard. "Like you didn't startle me with the phone?"

"Less threatening."

"What are you doing here?"

"You know I wasn't going to just let you hang up when I knew you were worried. Can I come in?"

She wanted to say no, but she knew he'd driven all the way from downtown Baltimore to see if she was all right.

"I'll open the door," she answered instead.

When she turned on the porch light, she saw him striding up the walk. A tall, attractive, well-built man dressed in jeans and a leather jacket, he looked like he owned the place, and in the darkness, he could have been Craig coming home late from an overtime assignment.

Except that Craig had been blond and green-eyed. Mack had dark hair and dark eyes. And probably dark stubble on his chin at this hour of the morning. Annoyed with herself for thinking of that, she stopped cataloging Mack's features and switched back to Craig. He was never coming home, and she'd better remember that.

She opened the door but didn't say, "Come in."

Taking the gesture as an invitation, Mack stepped into the front hall, then closed and locked the door behind him.

As he took off his coat and hung it on the antique hall tree, she felt emotions well up inside her. Emotions she didn't want to feel. He'd come here because he was worried, and she wanted to lean on his strength. At the same time, she wanted to tell him she was just fine on her own. But she'd proved just the opposite by making that call an hour ago.

When he turned back to her, tears sprang to her eyes, and she didn't know exactly where they came from. Maybe she didn't want to know.

"Sweetheart, what is it?"

She couldn't speak, couldn't resist when he reached for her and pulled her into his arms. She should duck away. Instead, with her eyes closed, she leaned against him, breathing in his scent, absorbing his strength. His hands stroked her back, her hair. It felt so good to be held after so long. *And not because it's Mack*, she told herself.

When his hands began to knead her tense muscles, she sighed and dropped her head to his shoulder. After Craig died, she'd worked hard to be self-sufficient. That resolve seemed to melt away as she nestled into the strength of Mack's arms.

Despite herself, she let a little fantasy play through her mind. If she lifted her head, he'd lower his, and their lips would meet. She could imagine what they felt like. Imagine what he tasted like.

The two of them swayed together, and she wondered if he was sharing a similar fantasy. If he—

She stopped her wayward thoughts and summoned the resolve to ease away.

"Don't," she whispered.

Instantly, his hands dropped to his sides.

Taking a step back, he dragged in a breath and let it out as he stood looking at her. While she tried to figure out what his expression meant, he said, "Tell me what's wrong."

Could she?

Talking to Jo had seemed like such a logical move. Talking to Mack didn't have the same appeal.

To keep from blurting anything right away she said, "Let's have a cup of tea."

"Okay."

He followed her into the kitchen and looked around in surprise at the flour, sugar and other ingredients spread around on the counter.

"You're baking?"

She flushed. "After we talked, I knew I wasn't going back to sleep, so I started making some of those baking jars we've been selling in the Lobby Shop."

"I see," he answered, though she was pretty sure the gift items weren't on his radar.

"They were selling so fast before Christmas that Sabrina asked me for some more," she answered. "She's paying me up front for the ingredients and giving me a commission on every sale. Maybe we can make them into a feature at the shop."

When she realized she was babbling, she stopped. Instead she asked, "What kind of tea do you want? Or would you prefer coffee?"

"Don't go to the trouble of making coffee. I'll have whatever you're having."

"You're into green tea flavored with ginger?"

"Maybe not. You got any... Earl Grey?"

There was a moment of silence when they both remembered that Craig had liked Earl Grey.

Turning quickly away, she filled the kettle and set it on a burner, then got tea bags out of the pantry and put them into mugs. As she waited for the water to boil, she finished up the jar she'd been making, then started putting away the rest of the supplies, aware all the time of Mack sitting at the kitchen table watching her. He didn't sit in Craig's chair, she noticed. Probably he knew which one to avoid.

As she wiped spilled flour from the counter, he said, "You'll feel better when you tell me why you called the office."

"Probably not."

"Give it a shot."

The kettle whistled, and she snatched it off the burner, then poured water into the mugs.

"Sugar?"

"No, thanks."

She added sugar to her own mug, keeping her back to him. After taking a breath and letting it out, she blurted, "I had a nightmare, and I think it's real."

"You mean, like you dreamed someone was outside, and you woke up and heard rustling in the shrubbery?" He glanced toward the darkened window. "Do you want me to check around the house now?"

"No. Not someone around here. Someone in Gaptown. Someone in trouble." She swallowed. "Someone who was calling out to me."

Long seconds passed before he answered. "That's your hometown?"

"Yes."

"They called on the phone?"

Obviously, he didn't get what she was trying to say.

More likely, she wasn't being very clear. She set his mug on the table in front of him but remained standing.

He shifted in his seat, keeping his eyes on her.

Her throat had turned dry, so that she had to swallow before she could speak. "Not a phone call or anything like that. It was a dream. But…I'm pretty sure it was real." Absolutely sure. But she wasn't going to say it that way. Not to Mack Steele.

He turned his mug around on the table. When he spoke, his words were measured. "Dreams aren't reality."

"Yeah. Right," she agreed too quickly. "Everybody knows that." Rushing on, she added, "It was a mistake for you to come over. I think the best thing for you to do is leave." As she spoke, she knew that her voice sounded sharper than she'd meant it to be.

ONE HUNDRED AND THIRTY miles away in Gaptown, Maryland, the man who now called himself Fred Hyde took off his fright mask and black cape. Still wearing a black shirt, pants and boots, he looked down at the lifeless body of the woman sprawled on the floor of the Funhouse.

Another one punished for her sins, even when she claimed not to know what she had done.

Her name was Lynn Vaughn, and she'd suffered before she'd died. Not so much physically, but mentally. He'd known how to feed her terror and enjoyed every moment that she'd run desperately through his private amusement park, trying to get away from the relentless pursuer behind her.

He'd told her more than once that she had a chance to escape, but that was just part of the fun for him. Really, he'd known all along how their private drama would end. Well, not which of his clever setups would stop her. But there was no question he would get her in the end, because that was his goal. When he set his mind to something, it always worked out the way he wanted.

He clenched his teeth. Except once. One damn time. In this damn town.

Asserting his will, he drove that thought from his mind. He would not think about failure. Not now.

He went back to contemplating his masterpiece. Everything had been planned. Down to the smallest detail. Like the place where the floor had been slippery. And then the hallway where she'd stubbed her toe on an unexpected rock sitting in the middle of the passageway. And it had all worked out the way he wanted. Yet…

He dragged in a deep breath and expelled it sharply. While she'd been running from him in terror, he'd had the strange feeling that someone else was watching the whole performance. Someone he couldn't see.

But that was impossible, of course. No one else was here. Not an invisible person or anyone else. Only himself and Lynn Vaughn. And he wasn't going to tell anyone what had happened to her. By the same token, she wasn't going to call up her friends and relate the nightmare either. He laughed at his little joke, then stopped abruptly.

Nightmare.

What was he thinking? Something impossible. Yet as unsettling thoughts swirled in his brain, he began to work faster, wrapping Lynn in the tarp he'd brought so she wouldn't get blood in his SUV. Methodically, he rolled up the body, which was still limp enough to handle easily, then carried her out the back door and down the steps to the detached garage.

When he'd deposited her in the back of the vehicle, he pulled down the long driveway and into the mist-shrouded city, heading for the mountains.

His sense of satisfaction increased as he began looking

for a good spot to dump the body. The ground was frozen, but he wasn't planning to dig a grave. He wanted people in this damn town to *know*.

He was going to make everyone who'd ruined his life four years ago pay for what they'd done. The punishment wouldn't make up for his loss, of course. But it would be fitting retribution. When he was finished, he'd leave this jerkwater town that was the scene of his misery and never come back.

MACK'S VOICE WAS FIRM when he spoke. "Jamie, I'm not leaving until you tell me why you called the Light Street Detective Agency at two in the morning."

Anger, anxiety and defiance warred within her. That was none of his damn business, but unfortunately she'd been too quick to make a phone call in the middle of the night, and he'd been the one on the other end of the line. She didn't owe him anything, yet she heard herself trying to justify her behavior.

"Like I said, I had a dream. A nightmare. It wasn't my dream, exactly. It was something happening to a woman in Gaptown."

He kept his gaze on her. "You're saying it was something that really happened?"

She swallowed hard before answering. "Yes,"

"How do you know?"

Chapter Two

Jamie wasn't going to start off by telling him she'd been plagued by psychic dreams since she'd been little. She was going to avoid that, if possible. And she wasn't going to explain that the dreams had stopped when she came to Baltimore with Craig.

Could she convince Mack with a concrete fact? Up till now, she'd avoided using a name, even in her thoughts, because that made the dream too real.

Now she raised her head and said, "The woman's name was Lynn Vaughn."

His instant alertness unnerved her. It was like when Craig was working on a case.

"How do you know?" he said.

"I just do."

"Maybe we'd better check that out."

"Okay," she whispered, wishing again that she'd kept her mouth shut. What was Mack thinking now? From the look on his face, she was pretty sure she wouldn't like his speculations.

"Where's your computer?" he asked.

"In the office." Craig's old office, which she'd kept looking like he'd left it so that when she sat at the desk she could pretend he was going to come to the door and ask her to get out of his chair.

She and Mack walked to the office, where Mack stopped for a moment in front of the desk before sitting down and booting up the machine. Jamie took the beat-up easy chair where she'd liked to sit and read while Craig was working in the evening. Usually he'd work late, and then they'd go upstairs and—

She ruthlessly cut off that line of thought. As Mack waited for the computer to go through the start-up routine, he said, "Lynn Vaughn, right?"

"Yes."

He brought up one of the programs you could use to locate people and typed in her name, plus "Gaptown."

Jamie sat with her pulse pounding, wondering if she had everything backward. What if it had been *her* dream, and she'd somehow pulled that woman into it? When Lynn Vaughn's listing came up, he dialed the number from his cell phone and put it on speaker so they could both hear. She sat clenching the arms of the chair as a woman answered on the first ring. It was the middle of the night, but obviously she wasn't sleeping.

"Lynn?" Mack asked.

"No. Who is this?"

"I'm an old friend of Lynn's. I was hoping to get in touch with her."

"At three in the morning?"

"Sorry. I didn't realize the time," he said, lying with the same facility that Craig had exhibited when he worked a case. "Is she there?"

Jamie could hear the tension in the woman's voice as she replied.

"Lynn didn't come home this evening, and she didn't call me. That's not like her. I'm worried."

"Have you called the police?"

"I—"

"You should do that," Mack said.

"What did you say your name was?" the woman asked.

Instead of answering, Mack clicked off and swung the chair around so that he could look at Jamie.

"Will she have your cell phone number on her caller ID?" Jamie asked.

He shook his head. "How did you know Lynn's name?"

She thought about how to answer. "I…don't know."

"And you don't have any specific information about her tonight?"

"What kind of information?"

He shrugged and kept his gaze on her.

"Like I told you, I had a dream," she repeated.

His reply totally startled her.

"I'm going to Gaptown in the morning."

Her own response was just as startling. "If you're going, I'm going, too."

"You don't need to do that."

"I'm not staying here if you're driving up there," she said, hearing her urgent tone and wishing she didn't feel compelled to return to the scene of so many unhappy memories before Craig had offered her an escape hatch.

She'd been taking classes at the local community college and working at the Star Bar and Grill when she'd met him. He'd come to town investigating an insurance fraud case in which a doctor had colluded with patients. Dr. Bradley had documented injuries after automobile accidents, injuries that he wrote up as much worse than they really were. The patient would get a nice insurance settlement, which he split with the doc.

The moment Craig had walked into the restaurant, she'd been attracted to him. They'd gotten to talking, and he'd told her he'd be in town for several days. He could have eaten at a lot of different places, but he kept coming back when he knew she'd be on shift.

He'd been out of his element and lonely. She'd been friendly, and they'd ended up getting something going. They'd had a lot in common. He was from a small town, too. In Ohio. Only he'd had a scholarship to one of the state colleges.

After he'd sewn up the case against the doctor, he'd had another job that had brought him back to town. And after that, he'd kept returning to visit her. She'd moved to Baltimore to be with him, and gotten a job in the shop at 43 Light Street with Sabrina Cassidy. Pretty soon after that, she and Craig had gotten married.

Because she'd been ambitious, she transferred her credits to UMBC. She'd just gotten her degree in history when Craig had gotten killed, and she'd canceled her law school plans. Better to wait awhile before getting back into serious studying again.

"I'm spending the night," Mack said, totally disrupting her thoughts.

Jamie blinked. "You certainly are not!"

Mack kept his gaze on her and his voice even. "I don't want to leave you alone tonight."

"Because you suspect I'm up to something illegal?"

"Of course not," he answered, too quickly for her taste. "You shouldn't be alone. That's all."

She stared at him, knowing that she wasn't strong enough to physically run him out of the house. She wasn't going to get Craig's gun and point it at him, either, but she didn't have to make this easy for him.

In a voice dripping with ice, she said, "If you want to sleep on the couch, go ahead." As she spoke, she remembered that the bed in the guest room had clean sheets, but she kept that to herself.

"Okay," he answered, his tone mild. "You go on up and I'll stay down here."

The fight knocked out of her for the moment, she turned her back to him and without another word, she walked out of the kitchen.

MACK WATCHED THE RIGID set of Jamie's shoulders as she exited the room. He was sure she hated having him here, but that wasn't going to make him back down. He was worried about her, and he was glad she hadn't put up too much of an argument. Still, she was being as inhospitable as possible. When she had climbed the stairs, he walked into the living room and looked at the couch, which wasn't exactly going to be comfortable for his six-foot-two frame. She hadn't even offered him a blanket, but an afghan lay along the upper edge of the backrest. He kicked off his shoes and arranged several small, square pillows behind his head. Then he unfolded the afghan and lay down, trying to adjust the covering so that it would warm both his feet and his shoulders.

Had Jamie taken her clothes off upstairs and gotten back into bed? Or was she lying on top of the covers in her jeans and plaid shirt? Craig's plaid shirt, actually.

He forced himself to stop thinking about what she was doing up there and focused on earlier in the evening. She'd been genuinely upset when she'd called the office. So what was going on?

Perhaps she really had some inside information on Lynn Vaughn, but didn't want to admit what she knew, so she'd made up the nightmare story to create an explanation.

He glanced at the stairs, then walked quietly back into the office where he sat down at the computer again. After another furtive glance at the door, he called up the secure database that Light Street used and accessed Jamie's phone records. As far as he could see, she hadn't made any calls to Gaptown in the past few weeks. And she hadn't received any, either.

Again he glanced at the door and listened for sounds of activity upstairs. After long moments of quiet, he opened Jamie's email and looked at her messages. Once more, he found nothing that had to do with the reason she'd called Light Street.

He breathed out a small sigh, relieved but feeling guilty about snooping.

Still, he'd like to know if she'd been back to Gaptown in the past few weeks.

He wished he could stop thinking and acting like a detective when it came to Jamie. She'd asked him if he thought she was up to something illegal. He didn't want to believe that, but the alternative didn't exactly make sense. Although she'd said she'd had a dream in which she watched something bad happen to Lynn Vaughn, she'd never spoken of any psychic experiences before, nor had Craig ever mentioned anything like that about his wife. But would he tell anyone else something that weird?

Mack couldn't help wondering if Jamie was stressed beyond the breaking point by her husband's death and then life on her own. Of course, he wasn't going to say that to her.

Trying to turn off his inconvenient thoughts, he returned to the living room, laid his weapon on the coffee table and lay down. Eyes closed, he courted sleep. It wasn't that easy with two little pillows under his head and his stocking feet sticking out onto the end table. But he finally dozed off.

In the morning he was startled awake by a crashing noise.

Springing off the sofa and reaching for his weapon, he looked for the source of the sound and saw a light in the kitchen. As he rushed in, gun in hand, he saw Jamie, dressed in jeans and a T-shirt, standing in front of the stove, where she was lighting a burner that held a heavy frying pan. Presumably, she'd just slammed the pan onto the burner by way of a cheery good morning gesture, leaving no doubt that she was still pissed at him.

She turned and gave him and the weapon a considering look. There was no need for her to ask how he'd slept because that was all too obvious—he'd tossed around in rumpled clothes most of the night.

He brushed back his hair and ran his tongue over his teeth. "I don't suppose you have an extra toothbrush?" he asked.

She waited several beats before taking pity on him. "In the medicine cabinet."

He went upstairs, used the facilities, then washed his face and brushed his teeth. After rubbing his dark stubble, he reopened the medicine cabinet and got out one of the pink disposable razors.

Her shaving cream was on the edge of the tub, and he used that, too, feeling guilty about taking liberties, but he was feeling more human when he came back down.

The smell of eggs, bacon and coffee drew him to the kitchen, where Jamie was moving briskly about, getting down plates. He could tell from her quick movements that she wanted to pitch him out of the house.

"Anything I can do to help?"

"I've got it under control."

He poured himself a mug of coffee, then helped himself to eggs from the pan and bacon from a plate sitting on the stove.

"Toast?" she asked.

"That's okay."

"Do you want it or not?" she snapped.

"No, thanks."

So much for civil conversation.

After she'd sat down across from him and taken a few bites of the eggs, he said, "You still want to come with me?"

"No."

"Good."

"But I'm going anyway. I think you're going to need me."

"What does that mean?"

"I guess we'll find out."

Half of him wished he hadn't been on duty last night, and the other half was glad that he had been there when she called, but he couldn't tell her that or much of anything else.

"Pack an overnight bag," he said.

"Why?"

"Because it's a long ride and we might not get back tonight."

"Fine." She ate a piece of bacon before asking, "What about you?"

"We'll stop at my house. I keep a bag packed."

She nodded, then got up and scraped the rest of her breakfast into the trash. He ate a few more bites, then cleaned off his own plate.

"I'm sorry," he said.

"About what?"

"Upsetting you."

She made a sound like *harrumph* and began cleaning the pan where she'd cooked the eggs, her shoulders rigid.

He turned away, went back to the living room and folded up the afghan.

"I'll be right back," she said over her shoulder as she climbed the stairs. When she was gone, he waited a moment, then pulled his cell phone from the holster on his belt and called the office.

Max Dakota answered. "Mack, I see from the log that you checked out last night. Where are you?"

"Something came up. I need to make a quick trip to Gaptown."

"Because?"

He shifted his weight from one foot to the other. "It's personal," he said, glad that Light Street detectives had a lot of freedom. Still, he held his breath until Max said, "Okay."

"I could be out for a couple of days," he added, just as Jamie stepped back into the living room and stopped short when she saw he was on the phone.

As she gave him a long look, he said, "I'll talk to you later."

"Who was that?"

"The office."

She kept her gaze on him as she asked, "Did you say you're driving a nut to Gaptown?"

"Of course not," he snapped, then changed the subject, striving for an even tone. "You packed fast."

"We're not going out dancing," she muttered.

"Yeah. Right.

"Do you want me to take out the trash?" he asked. "I mean, since you're going out of town."

She hesitated for a moment. "All right. The cans are by the back door."

He pulled the plastic bag out of the kitchen trash can and carried it outside. When he came back she was loudly shaking out a new bag, and he knew she was uncomfortable with him doing a job her husband had obviously taken care of when he'd been alive.

The little kitchen drama set the tone for the trip to western Maryland. After a quick stop at his house to pick up his bag, they headed down Route 70 toward Hagerstown, then onto Route 68 toward Gaptown—the supposed scene of her nightmare.

JAMIE SLID HER EYES toward Mack, then away as she sat in the front seat of his SUV, wondering what she was doing there. She could have stayed home, but she'd insisted on coming along, and once she'd committed herself to the trip, she'd known that he wasn't going to let her drive her own car.

Now she felt trapped in the front seat with Mack Steele, wishing she were anywhere else. What if the dream was something she'd conjured up out of her own anxiety? She'd be embarrassed that Mack was driving her all this way to check out a figment of her imagination, but that would be the end of it. Despite her mixed emotions, she clung to that hope as they drove west, the terrain becoming more hilly the farther they got from Baltimore. Her refuge. She'd established a life in the city, and she was going to keep living there.

Last week, she'd gotten a letter from her mother, asking her to come home for a visit. She'd ignored the request, because going home always stirred up the bad feelings between herself and her mother's boyfriend, Clark Landon, along with memories from her childhood that she'd rather forget.

Her earliest recollections of her father were of him staggering around the house drunk, yelling at her mom. Because of his fondness for the bottle, he'd barely been able to support the family with a series of jobs for the railroad, a couple of trucking companies and then as a delivery man for a local flower shop. Because home hadn't been a warm and comfortable place, she'd spent as much time elsewhere as she could. She'd haunted the library and gone home with friends after school. But the time would always come when she had to go back to the dilapidated bungalow where she lived. And she never knew what she was going to find there. Maybe her parents would be fighting. Or maybe Dad would be at one of the bars he frequented, and Mom would lock the door to keep him out. Then he might smash a window to get in and cut his hand and end up in the emergency room.

Dad had finally drunk himself to death before he was fifty, which had made home life calmer. They'd gone on welfare, which hadn't even made much difference in their lifestyle.

She'd still been living at home when she'd met Craig. Moving to Baltimore had been the first step in her break from the past. They'd had four good years together, and when he'd gotten killed, she'd been in danger of slipping into depression—until she'd pulled herself together and started over again on her own.

She'd thought she was in pretty good shape—until she'd woken up scared and shaken last night after a nightmare trip back to Gaptown.

The closer they got to home, the more her nerves jumped and the more certain she was that she wasn't going to like the outcome of this trip. Not at all.

"Slow down," she said. They were the first words she'd uttered since she'd gotten into Mack's car. "There's a speed trap ahead."

He pressed on the brake and they rounded a curve,

where a cop car with flashing lights had stopped another motorist.

"Thanks," he said. "Was that a psychic insight?"

"No," she snapped, then continued in a milder tone. "I'm a native. I know the cops are lying in wait for out-of-towners around that bend."

When she saw a highway sign coming up, she felt a little jolt as the exit name flashed by. Smokehouse Road.

"Take this exit," she said.

"Why?"

"Take it," she insisted.

"Why?" he asked again.

"I don't know for sure," she answered honestly. "But I think we're going to…find something."

She gripped the sides of her seat as he took the exit a little too fast. She wished she knew why she was giving him these directions. Or maybe she already knew, and she didn't want to admit it.

"Right or left?" he asked with an edge in his voice when they came off the exit ramp.

"Right," she answered, wondering why she was so certain where they were going. There was absolutely no hesitation on her part as she gave him directions.

They drove for a few more moments before she told him to turn onto Jumping Jack Road.

FROM A HIDING PLACE where he was sheltered by the woods, the man who called himself Fred Hyde took a bite of the caramel, nut and chocolate bar he'd brought along. He chewed with appreciation as he watched the activity down the hill through binoculars. All those cops rushing around looked like a bunch of ants serving their queen.

He laughed. Yeah, ants.

He'd considerately left the body where it was going

to be easily spotted—along the side of the road in a nice open valley. Then he'd made himself comfortable up here, waiting for the fuzz to show up and get to work. They'd be from Gaptown, but he knew there was a cooperative investigative unit that drew on some of the other surrounding jurisdiction.

He'd seen them find Lynn Vaughn's I.D., so they knew who she was, but they didn't know why she was here. And, of course, he'd worn rain gear that wouldn't leave any fibers on the body. He'd also moved the woman from his property to this location, so they weren't going to find any clues to his identity.

But he wanted them to understand that something serious was going on in their little town, with its speed traps and cops who were so quick to do their duty.

He would have liked to keep enjoying the show, but he had work to do. He took a last bite of the candy bar and crumpled the wrapper, but he wasn't dumb enough to drop the trash where someone could find it and maybe get a line on his DNA. Instead he put the crumpled paper into his pocket and started down the other side of the hill to where he'd left his car. Things were moving faster now. He had to set up the funhouse again to get ready for the next victim.

"NOW WHAT?" MACK CLIPPED out as he continued down the blacktop.

"Keep going," she directed, hardly able to speak around the tight feeling in her throat. Pictures were forming in her mind, but she thrust them away. She could be making them up. She hoped she was making them up.

He drove past a couple of farms and a country store.

"You know this area?"

"Of course. When I was in high school, my friends and I would come out here to drive around."

They didn't speak again until she saw a crossroads with a restaurant, bar and gas station.

"Turn left here."

He slowed the car and made the turn. From the small commercial area, they drove into the mountains, where they passed widely spaced farms and houses. When they rounded a steep curve, they were stopped by a police car with flashing lights blocking the road.

A few cars were pulled up along the shoulder, and several spectators were standing along the blacktop, craning their necks toward the center of the activity, where two more patrol cars were pulled up, along with an ambulance.

Mack rolled down the window and pulled up beside a man in jeans and a plaid shirt who was standing on the shoulder and staring toward the cop cars. "What's going on?"

"Guy found a woman's body."

Jamie had been hoping against hope not to hear that news. Now she dragged in a sharp breath as the words slammed into her.

"A local resident?" Mack asked.

"Don't know. The cops have been asking if we know a Lynn Vaughn. That must be her name."

Jamie felt a shiver go over her skin as her worst fears were confirmed. She'd been with Lynn Vaughn in her dream. She'd been afraid someone had killed the woman, and now she knew for certain it was true.

"You know her?" the guy asked, looking from Mack to Jamie and back again.

"No. We just happened down this road. I guess we'd better go back the other way," Mack answered easily, giving nothing away before he rolled up the window, made a U-turn and got them out of the vicinity. He kept going toward the road where they'd exited the highway, then turned into the parking lot of the country store they'd passed earlier. After finding a parking space, he cut the engine and turned to Jamie.

His face looked grim. "I thought maybe the dream came from your imagination," he said.

She lifted one shoulder. "Even after I gave you a name, and you confirmed that she was a real person?"

"Yeah."

"Maybe that's what you wanted to think, but I knew something had happened."

"You dreamed about a murder that turned out to be true…."

Somehow she managed to keep her voice even as she said, "I was hoping it didn't end that way."

His eyes boring into her, he said, "People don't dream about a murder one night, then find out the next day that it really happened."

Chapter Three

Jamie swallowed, wishing that Mack would stop using the word *murder* like a bludgeon.

"Tell me *exactly* what you dreamed."

She'd deliberately been vague with the details of the nightmare when she'd told him about it. Now she knew she was going to have to be more specific.

"Jamie?"

She stared straight ahead, her hands folded one on top of the other in her lap. "In the dream, I wasn't myself. I was that woman, Lynn Vaughn. She was in a…I guess you'd have to call it a funhouse."

"What do you mean by that?"

"Did you ever go to a haunted house on Halloween when you were a kid? Like maybe something set up by a local charity to raise money? They had a bunch of spooky stuff to give the kids a fright, but everybody knew it was all for fun."

"Yeah."

"It was like that, only it was serious." She clenched her hands together as she remembered the experience and the place. "It was dark and enclosed. There was scary music. A musty smell. Hallways with things set up to startle you, like witches jumping out. But some of it was a lot worse. One place had a trapdoor where she tumbled through and ended up on a slide that took her to the basement. She landed hard on the cement floor and hurt her shoulder."

Jamie winced, remembering the pain.

She hated dredging up more details, but Mack was staring at her with an expectant look on his face, so she gulped in a breath and let it out before she went on.

"The light was weird. Someone had worked hard to make the place into a creep show. In one section, there were horror movie posters. Dead-end hallways. Spatters on the floor that looked like blood.

"At first she was alone. But she kept hearing a man's voice coming from hidden speakers. Then he was *there*. With her."

Details came fast and furious now.

"He was wearing black clothes, a black cape, a hood, boots. His face was a mask with a skull. He was talking to her, telling her she was going to pay for what she'd done to him. But he was also telling her that if she could find her way out, he'd let her go. Then she came to a place where she could go right or left. She didn't want to go on, but he forced her to choose.

"When she did, bright lights went off in her face so she could hardly see, and he came at her with a knife. I don't think it would have mattered which way she went."

Jamie rushed on, wanting to get the recitation over with. "He slashed at her, and I felt her pain. Then everything went black. I was hoping she'd fainted, but I was afraid he'd killed her. I guess he did."

She said the last part with a little hitch in her voice as she turned to Mack, seeing the set lines of his face.

When he spoke, it was like he hadn't listened to anything she'd said. "Explain to me how you knew about what was happening to Lynn Vaughn."

She sighed, deep and loud. "It's what I said the first time. I dreamed about her."

"That's all? You didn't talk to anyone about her? Get some information from someone?"

"It was a dream!" She heard her voice rise.

"Just a dream. Out of the blue?"

The question made her want to open the door, jump out of the car and run down the road to get away from her interrogator, but she was pretty sure she wouldn't get very far. Mack would catch up with her and drag her back.

Instead, she raised her chin. Struggling to keep her voice steady, she said, "I used to have bad dreams when I lived in Gaptown. I'd have a nightmare and it would turn out to be true."

Before he could demand an example, she went on quickly. "It started when I was nine. I dreamed that Peggy Wickers, a girl in my fourth-grade class, was in an automobile accident. I woke up crying, and my mother came in to calm me down. She was angry that I'd gotten her up in the middle of the night. She told me it was just a nightmare and to go back to sleep. I lay there the rest of the night, thinking about it. Then in the morning, Peggy didn't come to school and the teacher told everyone about the accident."

She stopped to catch her breath, then went on. "I'd have dreams like that off and on. Sometimes one every six months, sometimes it wouldn't happen for a year. It was always something bad, and it always turned out to be true. It stopped when I moved to Baltimore, and I thought I was over it. Then last night, it happened again. I think it's because it was happening *here*."

"Uh-huh."

"Are you saying you don't believe me?"

"It's a pretty strange story."

"Why would I come up with something so weird if it wasn't true?"

"You tell me."

She exploded with an unladylike curse. "I told you everything I could."

"Why did you call the Light Street office in the middle of the night?"

She wasn't going to tell him that she'd awakened wishing her husband were lying beside her in bed. Instead she said, "I was upset when I woke up. I was hoping to talk to Jo. She wouldn't have put me through the third degree."

"She would have been remiss if she hadn't questioned you."

"She wouldn't have acted like I was part of a murder conspiracy!"

Mack sighed. "Okay."

"So you finally believe me?"

"Do I have a choice?"

Jamie heard herself saying words she thought she would never utter. "Why don't you drop me off at my mom's house. I'll catch a ride home on my own."

"We can visit your mom, but then we're going to try and figure out what happened to Lynn Vaughn. Where's the house?"

Feeling trapped, she gave him the address. Maybe she could slip out the back door and call one of her old friends in town while he was having a nice chat with the family. That thought made her bite back a sharp laugh. Yeah, Mom and Clark were going to charm the pants off Mack.

She felt her stomach knot as Mack put the address into his GPS. Apparently going to see Mom was as threatening as being questioned about a murder.

The place was at the south end of town—the low-rent district—and she gave the familiar location a critical look as they pulled up in front of the one-story bungalow. The lawn and shrubbery were scraggly, the porch sagged and paint was peeling from the wooden siding. Home sweet home.

Embarrassed that one of her friends from Baltimore was seeing this house, she climbed out and headed up the cracked sidewalk with Mack right behind her.

She thought about him as a friend, she realized. Maybe *associate* was more accurate. Or maybe they were playing detective and suspect.

At the front door, she stopped and knocked. From the corner of her eye she saw a curtain move in the dirty front window and guy with a ruddy face and thinning hair look out.

Clark Landon. Too bad Mom's boyfriend was there.

He opened the door and stared at Jamie.

"What's the Princess of Baltimore doing here?"

"Mom asked me to visit."

"But that's no reason for you to stop by, is it?" he shot back.

Mack cleared his throat. "I asked Jamie to show me around Gaptown."

Clark took notice of the man standing behind Jamie and straightened his shoulders. "And who the hell are you?"

"Mack Steele. A friend of Jamie's." He didn't say, "Nice to meet you."

If Mack hadn't been right behind her, she might have turned and left, but now she was trapped by her own bad idea.

"Hey, Gloria, you won't believe who's here. It's your hoity-toity daughter."

He stepped aside, and Jamie and Mack walked into the living room, which was cluttered with two beat-up sofas, an old-style clunky television set and beer cans on the maple coffee table. The brown carpet had turned several shades darker since Jamie had been home last. To the right, in the kitchen, the sink was piled with dirty dishes. The house smelled like cabbage that had been cooked a week ago and left out.

She shifted her weight from one foot to the other, wondering how she could have brought Mack here.

As they stood awkwardly in the middle of the room, Clark grabbed a corduroy car coat from a hook beside the door.

"I'm going down to Louie's," he said, then stepped out the door, slamming it behind him.

"Friendly," Mack muttered.

"He and I never got along."

"He's not your father, right?"

"Mom's longtime boyfriend."

She closed her mouth abruptly as Gloria Wheeler shuffled into the living room. Jamie tried to see her from Mack's point of view and took in a woman in her late fifties with graying hair dyed black-cat dark, a ruffled yellow blouse and beige polyester slacks, the outfit finished off with scuffed red slippers.

No hug. No kiss. And she didn't invite them to make themselves comfortable.

Mom just stood with her hands on her hips and gave Jamie a long look, then switched her gaze to Mack.

"I wasn't expecting you to drop by, and Clark sure didn't warn me that you had someone with you," she said in an accusing voice.

Jamie wondered what difference that made. Would Mom have rushed around cleaning up? Would she have had the table set so she could offer them tea and cookies? Or maybe she'd have changed her clothes and put on real shoes before coming out here.

"We were in town," Mack said, "and Jamie mentioned that she wanted to stop by."

"In town for what?"

"I'm a private detective on a case. Since Jamie's from here, I asked her to show me around Gaptown, Mrs....?"

"Wheeler," she supplied as she looked Mack up and down, then switched her gaze back to her daughter.

"You've taken up with another detective?"

Jamie answered in a rush. "I haven't taken up with him."

"I was a friend of Jamie's husband, Craig," Mack said.

Mom's knowing smile made Jamie cringe. What did she think? That they were sleeping together?

"I guess it was a bad idea coming here," she said.

Gloria shrugged. "You said it, not me. You too good for Gaptown now?"

Unable to contain her exasperation, Jamie asked quickly, "If you didn't want me here, why did you write to me?"

Gloria tipped her head to one side, considering. "I didn't write you."

"But I got a letter from you last week."

Gloria's voice hardened. "Not from me you didn't."

Jamie swallowed, wondering why her mother was lying, but she knew from experience that making a point of it wasn't going to get her anywhere. "I guess this was a mistake," she murmured. "We won't take up any more of your time."

"Suits me."

Without waiting for Mack, Jamie turned and fled the house. On the porch she took a deep breath. Behind her, she heard him say, "Nice to meet you, Mrs. Wheeler."

Yeah, sure.

Then he was hurrying after her down the sidewalk.

When she'd climbed into the car, she kept her gaze down as she fumbled with her seat belt. Her hand was shaking, but she finally got it hooked.

"I'm sorry," she whispered. "It was obviously a mistake dropping in there."

"Yeah." He pulled away from the curb, and they rode in silence for a few moments until Mack cleared his throat. "Was your mom like that when you were little?"

"Like what?"

"Mean. Self-centered. And not much interested in keeping her house or herself neat."

"She was never much for housework, but she wasn't so mean when I was little. I think she started reacting to her life."

"Some people cope better than others."

"She's a very dependent woman who can't function without a man to take care of her. Not that Clark Landon does much for her. My dad drank. She couldn't leave him either. After he died, she went looking for another man and ended up with Landon, unfortunately."

She sat tensely in her seat, expecting some kind of cutting remark about Gloria from Mack. Instead he pulled up along the curb, under the branches of a maple tree and turned toward her.

"I understand better than you think. My home life was no sitcom, either."

That surprised her. "What do you mean?"

He laughed, the sound low and rough. "From what I can pick up on short acquaintance with Gloria, I guess my mom was the polar opposite of yours. When I was ten, she decided that she was tired of taking care of a husband and two kids. One day my older brother and I came home from school, and she wasn't there. We went looking for her and found out she'd cleared out the clothes she wanted and left the rest for Goodwill.

"There was a note on the kitchen counter telling my dad not to try and contact her, and that she'd taken her share of the money in their bank account—which turned out to be most of it, since she said she'd been an unpaid housekeeper for years. That was the last we heard from her." He sighed. "I don't actually know if she's dead or alive. I guess, being a detective and all, I could investigate and find out, but it doesn't seem worth it."

"I'm sorry," Jamie murmured as she tried to imagine what his childhood must have been like.

"Yeah, well, I guess neither one of us had the pleasure of growing up in a stable home. After she bailed out on us, Dad did the best he could, but he had to work, which left me and Sammy on our own a lot of the time. At least there was an upside. It made me self-sufficient. I learned to cook and do my own laundry. And I can sew on a button, come to that."

Jamie searched his face, touched that he'd revealed so much to her when he could have simply kept silent. She'd always thought of him as stable and grounded, and now he was letting her know that he'd overcome some serious obstacles. He was doing something else as well. Trying to help her understand that his visit to her family hadn't shocked him. She appreciated the effort.

She'd been through an emotional wringer during the past twenty hours, and the glimpse into his unhappy background made her want to...

What? Thank him for revealing himself? Or maybe the wounded look in his eyes made her want to let him know that everything was all right. Whatever that meant.

Without fully understanding her own motives, she reached for him and pulled him close.

She'd felt safe in his arms last night when he'd come rushing over to find out what was wrong, and she'd never thanked him for that. She'd only bristled at the questions his job had compelled him to ask.

Suddenly, everything had shifted. When she eased back and tipped her face up, she found that her mouth was only inches from his. It had been a long time since she'd kissed a man, and she'd be fooling herself if she tried to deny that she'd thought of kissing *this* man. For heartbeats, neither one of them moved, except for their shallow breathing. It wasn't too late to stop. Somewhere in her mind she knew she should pull away, but she stayed where she was for a charged second and then another.

She wasn't sure which of them moved to close the gap, maybe both of them.

"Jamie." He said her name as their mouths met, and he moved his lips over hers in a kiss that was tender and needy and sexy, all at the same time.

Wanting to shut out the world, she closed her eyes so that she could focus on the man who held her in his arms.

She liked the taste of him. The texture of his lips. The heat of his body. Without even thinking about what she was doing, she felt her arms encircle his neck. In response, he gathered her closer as he turned his head first one way and then the other to change the angle of the kiss.

Somewhere in her mind, a voice spoke. This is wrong. You shouldn't be in his arms. You shouldn't be kissing him. But it was impossible to heed that voice when it felt like the most natural thing in the world to be close to him like this. As she nestled in his embrace, she could imagine what it would be like to share more than this kiss with him. Not just a sexual encounter but all the emotions she'd kept bottled up inside her for long, lonely months.

His tongue played with the seam of her lips, asking her to open for him, and she did, so that he could explore the line of her teeth, then stroke the sensitive tissue on the inside of her lips.

She made a small sound deep in her throat, telling him she liked what he was doing. When his tongue dipped farther into her mouth, hot, needy sensations curled through her body.

His hands stroked up and down her ribs, gliding upward to find the sides of her breasts, making her nipples tighten. She wanted to beg for more. She'd forgotten where they were. Forgotten why she shouldn't allow this man such liberties.

She tangled her hands in his thick, dark hair, loving the slightly rough texture. For months she'd wanted to touch him there, and now she had the freedom to do it. Sensations she hadn't experienced for too long bombarded her body and overwhelmed her mind.

Wanting more of him, she eased back a little so that she could pull open the front of his leather jacket and press her hands against his broad chest.

"Yes," he murmured, his mouth still on hers.

She rubbed her hands against him, feeling hair crinkle through his shirt. It would be dark and thick and textured like the hair on his head.

Through the fabric, she found a flat nipple, feeling it stiffen at her touch. Her other hand found the placket of his shirt. When she slipped two fingers inside, he dragged in a sharp breath.

Her own nipples had tightened painfully, and she pictured herself dragging his hand to her breasts. Before she could do it, the sound of a car horn intruded into the fog of her brain.

Jerking away from Mack, she looked wildly around and

saw a pickup truck pulling into the driveway just ahead of them. An old guy behind the wheel was glaring at them like they'd been filming a porn movie in the street.

Mack cursed under his breath and started the engine. The car bucked as he pulled away from the curb.

Jamie flopped back into her seat, fumbling with the seat belt, her face hot.

"Sorry," he muttered as he put distance between themselves and the homeowner.

She made some kind of sound that could have been agreement or condemnation. It would be easy to accuse him of taking advantage of her, but she knew that it wasn't true. She'd been a willing participant in what they'd been doing, and she wasn't even sure how far they would have gone if they hadn't been interrupted.

She might have admitted as much, but his next words sent her mind spinning off in an entirely different direction.

"There are some things you didn't tell me about Lynn Vaughn's murder," he said as he put distance between themselves and the guy who'd so rudely knocked them out of whatever fantasy they'd been sharing.

"Oh great. You can't deal with kissing me, so you're switching back to Lynn Vaughn?" she said, hearing the grating sound of her own voice.

"Can you?" he asked.

He had a point. She'd ended up in his arms with very little provocation, and she'd started touching him in ways that were totally inappropriate. She had no excuse for that, other than her own emotional instability.

She sighed. "Okay, we can get back to business. What do you want to know?"

"You told me that you'd have dreams about bad things

happening to people you knew, and they'd turn out to be true."

"Yes."

"Are you saying that you knew Lynn Vaughn?"

The question had edged into territory she didn't want to explore with him. "Why do we have to keep talking about this?"

"Because I'm going to have to call the police if we don't."

Chapter Four

The threat had the effect Mack must have been striving for. "I didn't say it, but I did know her. She and I went to high school together."

"Why didn't you tell me that?"

"It wasn't relevant."

He looked at her, then turned back to the road. "It could be. Any detail could be."

When she said nothing, he asked, "Were you close?"

She sighed. "We weren't best buddies, but we knew each other. I know that when she graduated, she went to the University of Maryland in Baltimore. She became an emergency room nurse."

"Did you keep in touch with her?"

"No. I kind of avoided Gaptown. I think you can figure out why."

"Yeah. But why do you think Lynn reached out to you? Did she know about your dreams?"

"I didn't advertise it. Nobody knew. Except Mom."

"Would she tell anyone?"

"She kept it between us, because she didn't want people to know there was something weird about her daughter."

A FEW MILES AWAY, Fred Hyde was touring the funhouse making sure everything was ready for the evening's entertainment. He'd had a very satisfying time selecting the exhibits. He'd used some of the same ones as for his last guest. Others were new, and he'd taken down the funhouse mirrors. Those were too much of a cliché. Now he was trying to decide if he was going to use a witch's face or a demon for the pop-up display on the first floor.

The witch had worked very well. But it might be amusing to give the green-and-purple-faced demon a try.

Still pondering the choice, he went back through his music selections, most of which he'd pulled from the soundtracks of slasher movies, although he also liked that spooky "Night on Bald Mountain." He'd mixed and matched the tracks, and he hummed along as he listened to some of the cuts, then decided on the disc that started with the *Night of the Living Dead* and continued on to *The Texas Chainsaw Massacre*.

After he'd satisfied himself with the preparations, he went downstairs to look at the woman who was sleeping in the cell he'd constructed in the basement. He'd built the walls of cinder block, and the door was reinforced, so there was no chance of escape.

The woman on the narrow bunk inside was lying on her back, her blond hair fallen across her cheek. As he stood over her, he suppressed the urge to brush it back.

Better not touch her until he was wearing his gloves and his Locard suit. Well, it wasn't anything official. That's what he called it. Locard was the French forensic scientist who'd first pointed out that when two objects touched, each would leave traces of themselves on the other. But that wasn't going to happen with his suit made out of neoprene.

He took a step back, still staring at the sleeping woman. He'd drugged her, and she wasn't going to wake up for several hours. Plenty of time for him to go out to dinner, then put on his outfit. He'd be wearing it when he let her out of the cell, and then the games would begin. Of course, there might be fibers from the cape. But that didn't matter. He'd bought it at a vintage clothing store in Boston, so nobody was going to connect it with murders in western Maryland.

After making sure the door to the cell and also all the doors to the house were locked, he climbed into his SUV and drove to an area down by the Potomac River where there were some shops, artists' studios and restaurants. The Chamber of Commerce or some other group was sprucing up the town, but they'd left some major messes. Right down by the river was a half-demolished brick building that used to be a dye works. It dragged down the whole area. And there should be more restaurants to choose from. He'd had Italian for dinner last time before the fun. This time he was going to try that place where you could get Maryland crabcakes and barbecued ribs.

MACK HAD CONTINUED DRIVING as they talked, and Jamie looked up to see that they were on a road that ran parallel to the CSX train yard where more than a hundred freight cars were parked.

"Where are we going?"

"You said the funhouse was in Gaptown. Maybe we can find it."

"Gaptown's a big place."

"Not like say, Baltimore or Washington. Maybe you'll have some…insights."

"Okay." She took in a sharp breath.

"What?"

"I do remember hearing a train whistle in my dream."

"Which means it could be down here."

"No. The train goes right through town. There are even

bridges over the tracks on the west side—the elegant part of town. You can't get away from CSX. The railroad's been here since before the company bought the Chesapeake & Ohio."

"Then which way should we go?"

"You know more about murder than I do. Would the guy leave the body somewhere near the house, or would he drive far away?"

"Far away. Unless he wanted the cops nosing around his playground."

"Then we might as well head west, into the mountains."

He did as she asked, and they drove into the countryside. She looked at houses, but nothing seemed right. They were all too small and modern. Unless he had an enormous underground complex. No, that didn't seem right, since she remembered climbing upstairs.

"It's got to be bigger," she murmured. "There were lots of rooms. Lots of corridors. He must have modified the interior himself."

"We could try a development of tract mansions," he suggested.

"It's not a new house."

"How do you know?"

She thought about her impressions. "The floorboards were old. And some of the walls were real plaster. I guess drywall and plywood were added to make all those hallways."

"Okay.

"So how did Lynn get there?"

"I don't know."

"Either she drove herself there, or the killer drove her."

"Why would she drive herself?"

"Because she knew him and felt he wasn't a threat. Do you have any idea what kind of car he had?"

"No."

"I guess an emergency room nurse wouldn't moonlight selling any kind of products," he mused.

"She might. Something like cosmetics. Or cleaning supplies for one of those big companies that rope in a lot of owners. But she'd sell them to people she knew at work or at church, not door to door."

"I guess that's right." He thought for a moment. "You said the dream started when she was already in the house."

"I jumped into it when she was running from him. I had the impression that the…game had been going on for a while."

They drove through the countryside for almost an hour until Jamie said, "This is just wasting time. I didn't see the outside of the place. I'm not going to find it this way."

"I guess we might as well head back to town."

Since she had spent most of the previous night tossing and turning, she leaned back and closed her eyes, drifting off to sleep. Her eyes snapped open again when she felt the car stop.

"Where are we?"

"A hotel."

They were under a marquee, and she looked to her right, into the lobby of a multi-story upscale establishment that commanded a large plot of land near the old C&O canal and the river. Swinging her head back toward Mack, she said, "Surely you don't expect me to stay in a hotel with you?" She could have added, "After that kiss," but she left that part unspoken.

"I'm not going to come on to you, if that's what you

mean," he snapped, revealing that he wasn't as relaxed as he looked. "We'll get our own rooms."

"That's too expensive," Jamie protested.

"Expense account."

"Are you saying you're charging the Light Street Detective Agency for this trip?"

"I can do that, yeah."

"Who's your client?"

"The wife of a deceased colleague."

She stared at him. "Wait a minute, I didn't ask for you to go that far."

"There's no charge when we do jobs for each other. You included. We have special funds set aside."

"I don't want Light Street involved."

He shook his head. "You called us," he reminded her. "Which meant that you couldn't…didn't want to handle it by yourself. And you could be in trouble. I'm not letting this go."

Of course, he was right. She had called because she'd known she had to tell someone about the nightmare, but she hadn't let her thinking process carry her beyond that when she'd picked up the phone. She simply hadn't wanted to be alone with her own fears in the middle of the night.

They walked into the comfortably furnished lobby together, and Mack asked about two adjoining rooms. When he found out he could get a junior suite for less money, he took that.

The sixth-floor suite consisted of a bedroom and a living room with a fold-out couch.

"I thought it would be two bedrooms," she said, as she checked out the arrangements.

"You can have the bedroom. I'll take the sofa."

Feeling trapped, she nodded.

"We'll relax for a while. Then we can go out to eat or order in."

"Let me think about it." She turned and walked into the bedroom, closing the door firmly behind her, wishing she had her own car so she could go back home. Only maybe that wasn't such a great idea.

At the time she'd called the agency, she'd told herself she didn't know for sure what had happened to Lynn Vaughn. Now she knew Lynn was dead, and she couldn't just walk away. But why did she have to be stuck with Mack Steele?

When she pulled back the covers and lay down on the bed, her mind flashed back to the incident in the car. She wasn't going to kid herself about that. She was attracted to him, and she'd responded to his kiss, even when it never should have happened. Unfortunately, now they were going to be in each other's pockets.

At least she could stay in this room for the time being and keep away from him.

She closed her eyes, thinking that she was much too jumpy to relax. But the tense hours last night had taken their toll, and after a few minutes, sleep claimed her.

IN THE SITTING ROOM of the suite, Mack walked back and forth across the carpet, wondering what the hell he had gotten himself into. Kissing Jamie had been a big mistake. But it had happened, and now he had to deal with it, because it confirmed what he'd known all along. They were attracted to each other. The kiss had proved beyond a doubt that the chemistry was there. He sure as hell hadn't been the only one responding. She'd been as into it as he had. Although that didn't mean they'd suddenly both made up new rules for the relationship.

He clenched and unclenched his fists. He'd been fighting

his attraction to her, but what was wrong with getting involved, damn it? Her husband was dead. She wasn't cheating on him by starting a relationship with someone else. Only both of them obviously thought otherwise. Could he get over his guilt about going after Craig's wife? Could she stop thinking of herself as a married woman? He didn't know if either one of them could handle the relationship, and he had another problem.

Jamie had knowledge of a murder. She'd claimed to have gotten it through some kind of psychic dream. But could he believe it?

He knew some pretty weird things had happened to some of the Light Street staff and also to the men and women who worked for their sister organization, Randolph Security. He'd never gotten involved in anything he'd call extrasensory. Now he was caught between doubting Jamie's account and wondering if he could believe something that wasn't grounded in any reality he understood. He'd like to consult someone at the office. Jamie had been trying to get in touch with Jo O'Malley, and he knew that something paranormal had happened to her and her husband, Cam Randolph, years ago. But talking to his boss about the woman who'd closed herself in the other room would make him feel like a snitch.

He sighed. It seemed like he was caught in a trap. He didn't love being forced to explore his own feelings. At the same time, he couldn't simply walk away from a murder investigation. He could turn the problem over to someone else at Light Street, but that would mean he'd have to come up with a good reason for ducking out.

Since he wasn't prepared to do that, he was stuck for the moment. As he saw it, his only option was to investigate the murder the way he'd investigate any other case. Which made the expense account perfectly appropriate.

He turned on the television, keeping the sound low as he scanned for local news. Apparently there wasn't a station right in Gaptown, but there seemed to be two in a city about sixty miles away. And both of them had sent reporters here.

As he watched, he noted that the police hadn't released Lynn Vaughn's name yet, but he knew they were going to be interviewing her colleagues at work and her neighbors. Could he duplicate their research? And would the people he talked to wonder why he wasn't working with the cops? He'd started out on the Columbus, Ohio, police force. But he'd been caught in a personnel reduction. Since he had no seniority, he'd been let go. But Jo O'Malley, from Light Street, had been on a recruiting trip, and she'd offered him a job. He'd been with them for five years, and he loved the job.

When he'd watched the same news report several times without learning anything more, he knew he was just spinning his wheels.

After turning down the sound on the TV, he got out his laptop and checked his mail. There was nothing urgent, and nothing on the Net about the murder that he hadn't already seen on TV.

He closed the laptop and left it on the desk, then looked toward the bedroom. He'd given Jamie some space. Now it was time to get some dinner, turn in and start fresh in the morning.

He crossed the room, hesitated for a moment, then knocked on her door.

When she didn't answer he knocked again. "Jamie?"

Still no answer.

He twisted the knob and pushed the door open. The light was off, and it took his eyes a moment to adjust to the darkness. When they did, he saw Jamie lying on the bed. Her eyes were closed, and her breathing was regular. He walked closer, seeing that her lips were slightly parted. They looked so damn kissable. Quickly he flicked his gaze away, where it landed on her breasts as they rose and fell. She was sleeping and totally vulnerable to him. He could look at her in a way he'd never done when she was awake.

Only it wasn't any fun because he felt an immediate sense of guilt at invading her privacy. He caught his breath, then backed out of the room, closing the door behind him.

Obviously, she was worn out. She'd hardly slept the night before, and he wasn't going to wake her to go out to dinner, but he could bring back something they'd both like.

The question made him realize how little he knew about her tastes. But he remembered a Light Street Fourth of July party where he'd seen her eating ribs and buffalo wings. Something like that was probably safe.

The hotel had a binder with information on local restaurants. He found there was a place down by the river where you could get ribs and crabcakes. Kind of a weird combination, but it looked like he could walk down a path along the canal and get there in a few minutes.

In case Jamie woke up and wondered where he was, he wrote her a note explaining that he'd gone out to get them dinner. He left the sheet of paper on the rug where she'd be sure to see it if she stepped out of the bedroom.

Then he stopped at the desk to make sure he knew which way to walk. On the way to the restaurant, he passed an old dye works that was partly demolished. Too bad it was sitting right down in the tourist section of town. But maybe they could use the part that was still standing for shops or something.

Inside the restaurant, he grabbed a menu and scanned the selections. The cream of crab soup sounded good. He asked for two cartons and two orders of barbecued ribs. And salad. Women always liked salad.

While he waited for the kitchen to prepare the food, he looked around the restaurant and found a rack near the door with local newspapers. Maybe they'd give him some information that would help lead to the funhouse.

As he turned from the rack, he saw a man at a corner table watching him. The guy was pretty ordinary looking, but there was something unsettling about him.

Mack took in details. The guy was sitting down, but from the way he filled the chair, he was probably about six feet tall. He looked to be in his mid-thirties, with dark hair. Dark eyes. Wire-rimmed glasses. He was wearing a blue flannel shirt, hiking boots and dark slacks.

When he caught Mack scrutinizing him, he bent to his plate of crabcakes.

"Your order's ready," the woman behind the counter called out, and Mack turned away to get the food. When he'd paid with his credit card, he took one more look at the guy in the corner and saw he was now reading an outdoor magazine.

Mack exited the restaurant and took the path back to the hotel. When he walked into the room with their dinner, Jamie was sitting on the couch watching a recap of the earlier newscasts.

She used the remote to turn off the television and silence rang in the room.

"You're up," he said, thinking that was a pretty dumb line. "How are you feeling?"

"Rested."

He set the bags down on the coffee table. "Sorry. I

forgot to get drinks. But we can grab something from the minibar."

She got up and crossed the room, opening the little refrigerator. "What do you want?"

"Do they have Dr Pepper?"

She laughed. "That's your soft drink of choice?"

"Yeah."

She got out two cans of Dr Pepper and brought them to the table.

"You, too?"

She nodded. "Yes. I hate to find we've got something in common."

"Why?"

The question hung in the air between them. When she didn't answer, he sat down and gestured toward the food, as he told her what he'd gotten.

"There's only one place in town where you could have scored that combination."

She reached into one of the bags and took out the cartons, not hesitating to spoon up some of the soup. "I haven't had this in a while. It's as good as you can get in Baltimore."

He took the chair across from her, pulling it closer to the table.

After taking a spoonful, he nodded. "It's strange to specialize in crab when you're this far from the ocean."

"Uh-huh."

It was an oddly polite and cautious conversation. A few hours ago, they'd gotten intimate too fast. Now they were both backing off.

He wasn't sure how to get comfortable with her. She was obviously having similar thoughts, because she didn't offer any other topics of conversation, so they ended up eating most of the meal in silence.

After she'd eaten about half of her soup, ribs and salad, she got up and went into the bedroom, leaving him to clean up the trash, then open up the sleep sofa.

It wasn't the most comfortable bed he'd ever lain on, and it didn't make it any easier to sleep when he kept thinking about the woman in the next room.

JAMIE TOOK A SHOWER, then pulled on a long T-shirt over her panties and climbed into bed. There was another television in the bedroom, and she turned it on, flipping through the channels to find the local news. It was the same information she'd heard before. Nothing new. Yet she couldn't shake the conviction that there was something about to happen. Something she wasn't going to like.

Another dream?

She shuddered. She didn't want to dream about Lynn Vaughn again. And why should she? Lynn was dead.

Still, to keep herself awake, she kept pressing the buttons on the remote, finally finding an old movie that she'd seen before, but it was something to keep her mind off the man in the next room and the growing unrest that was making her chest tighten. She kept the television on past midnight, then worried she was going to keep Mack awake. When she finally flipped off the set, she was wrung out.

When she slid down under the covers, sleep claimed her easily. For a little while, she was at peace. Then the dream that had been hovering at the edge of her consciousness since she'd climbed into bed grabbed her by the throat and made her gasp.

She was back in the funhouse, running down a dark corridor, the breath sawing in and out of her lungs as she tried to get away from the man who had brought her here.

He'd drugged her and left her in a cell. She remembered that part. Then he'd told her to wake up and play the game he'd planned for the two of them. He'd said it was going to be fun. She'd known from the tone of his voice that he was lying.

It was deadly serious. For both of them.

He was behind her again, letting her get far enough away for her to hope that she could escape. Then he'd catch up with her the way he had before.

For Jamie, it was a replay of the previous trip through the funhouse. Only this time, it wasn't Lynn Vaughn. She was sharing another woman's thoughts and panic gripped her when she realized she had no idea who the woman was.

That had never happened to her before. When she'd had dreams before, they were always about a person she knew, a friend or someone from school. But even as she struggled to figure out who it was, she could detect no sense of familiarity. She didn't know this woman. Yet something tied them together, something she didn't want to examine too closely.

She longed to wake herself up, to escape from the funhouse and the man behind her, but deep in her heart she knew that would be taking the coward's way out. She must find out what was happening and who the man was.

That sense of purpose kept her tangled in the dream, kept her running for her life down a narrow corridor in the same house where she'd been the night before.

She had seen some of these traps in her previous visit, only there were new variations. The night before a witch had come flying down from the ceiling on a broomstick, screaming as she went. Tonight it was a green-faced monster.

Other elements were completely new. The woman came to a place where the corridor opened into a small room. She stopped short, trying to decide what to do next. There were three exits, and when she stepped toward one, a sizzling sensation zapped her nerve endings, making her scream. She jumped back, bumping into something swinging in the air. Whirling, she found it was a hangman's noose.

"No," she cried out, backing away, hitting another place on the floor where a live electric wire lurked. Again pain surged through her body. She screamed and wanted to keep screaming and screaming. But what good would that do? Teeth clenched, she ordered herself to calm down and think.

He had said she could get out of here. All she had to was find the exit.

Her heart pounding, she looked around, then chose the middle exit from the room. As she stepped through the door, the wooden floor gave way beneath her, and she tumbled through space, landing on a cold cement surface that rattled her bones. When she could finally breathe again, she pushed herself up, sending terrible pain shooting through her arm.

Reaching out in her mind, Jamie tried to say something reassuring. But the other woman couldn't hear her. Apparently, the communication only went one way.

Still, the woman's thoughts and her terror pounded her.

She held her injured arm against her chest, trying to ease the pain.

"Don't let it slow you down," she warned herself as she took a moment to rest. She was in a cellar, with cobwebs hanging from the ceiling. When she stretched out her foot, her shoe dipped into something slimy, and she stifled a scream.

After wiping her shoe against the floor, she looked up and saw something that made the blood freeze in her veins.

A man was peering at her through the hole in the ceiling where she'd come tumbling down.

It was him. Dressed in black with a death mask instead of a face.

"Why are you doing this to me?" she gasped out, still cradling her arm.

A moment ago, the man had been above her. Suddenly, his grating voice came from behind her. Had he taken another way to the basement? Or was the voice coming from a speaker?

"You know."

"I don't! Please. Just let me go."

"You ruined my life. You and the others. You took away everything from me."

"I don't know what you're talking about. Please. Let me go."

"If you can get out of here."

Ignoring the pain in her arm, she started running again, desperate for an escape route. When she spotted a flight of stairs leading upward, she almost sobbed in relief. If she could get out of the basement, maybe she could find her way out of the house.

As she dashed toward the steps, she stumbled over something lying in her path and almost lost her footing.

It looked like the dead body of a woman, her hair spread out across the cold basement floor and a knife sticking out of her chest.

His last victim? Jamie knew that couldn't be true because the police had discovered Lynn Vaughn along the road. The other woman must not have connected that case to this killer, this house. Or maybe she didn't even know about it.

Righting herself, she made it to the stairs and began scrambling up. She could hear his breathing, feel it on her neck. His hand came down on her shoulder, and he shook her.

"Wake up."

"No!" she screamed, struggling to get away.

Chapter Five

"Jamie. Wake up, Jamie."

She tried to dodge away, but it was no good. He held her fast.

She struck out with her fist, connecting with a hard body.

"Jamie, don't. It's Mack."

Her eyes blinked open. In the light coming from the sitting room, she found herself staring into Mack Steele's tense features.

"What happened?" he asked.

"Another dream," she managed to say through chattering teeth. She was cold all the way to the bone, although she was under the covers and the room was warm.

She couldn't stop shaking, and when he gathered her in his arms, she clung to him. Part of her mind was aware that his shoulders and chest were bare. He wasn't wearing a shirt, but she saw his denim-clad legs. Either he'd been sleeping in his jeans or he'd pulled them on before running in here.

"What happened?" he asked again.

She turned her head to the side, pressing her cheek to the pillow. "I don't want to talk about it."

"All right," he answered, but she knew that the reprieve

was only temporary. He was going to make her tell him about it, because he wasn't the kind of guy to let this go.

"Not now. Please. Not now," she protested.

"It's okay. You're okay."

Was she?

They were in a hotel room. Far from the funhouse. She should be safe here. She wanted to feel safe. Even more than that, she wanted to feel normal, and the most normal thing she could cling to was the man who held her in his arms. He was solid and strong. Sure of his own values. She'd always liked that about him, even when she'd understood that those values were keeping them apart as much as her own resolve.

A resolve that had apparently melted away. She'd reached for him once—and she needed to do it again.

Unable to stop herself, she lifted her face at the same time she clasped the back of his head and brought his mouth to hers.

After resisting for a moment, he covered her lips with his. The first kiss they'd shared in the car had been tender. That wasn't what she needed now. She needed to wipe out the memories of the awful dream. The moment his mouth touched down on hers, she moved her lips against his with a desperation that surprised her.

She was under the covers and he was above them, but she felt his weight shift, felt him stretch out beside her on the bed so that he could gather her close. As she clung to him, she closed her eyes, wanting him to be the only part of her reality that mattered.

She stroked his naked back, then downward until she encountered the waistband of his jeans.

He shifted again, drawing away, and she was afraid he was going to leave her. Instead he pulled down the covers to her waist so that he could gather her more tightly against his broad chest.

She burrowed into his warmth, loving the corded strength of his arms and the large hands that stroked over her shoulders and down her spine, sending shivers over her skin and deeper. When he brought his mouth back to hers, her tongue flicked out to play with his lips, then darted back, inviting him to follow. He did, stroking the inside of her lips, her teeth, the side of her tongue, sending currents of sensation through her.

It had been so long since she'd lain in bed with a man. As he kissed her and stroked her arms, she rediscovered sensations she'd forgotten existed.

With dreamy deliberation, she raised her hand, tracing a path along his cheek, loving the way the scratchy stubble contrasted with the softness of his lips moving over hers. His beard prickled at her nerve endings, raising the heat level of her whole body.

When her hand trailed to the side of his neck, she could feel his pulse accelerate. His response was like a secret jolt of power that fueled her own need.

He raised his head, staring down at her, and she felt her lips curve into a smile before she brought his mouth back to hers so she could deepen the contact, drinking in the wonderful taste of him.

She understood that he wasn't going to be the one to push things any further, but she needed more. Her breasts were full and achy now, and she had to feel his hands there. She found one and pulled it to her breast, cupping his palm around it, pressing her taut nipple against him.

He made a low sound as his other hand came up to join the first so that he could lift and squeeze her breasts gently, wringing a cry of satisfaction from her.

What he was doing felt so good that she was lost in a

swirl of sensations. Restlessly, she moved the lower part of her body against his, feeling his erection through the layers of fabric that separated them.

He was half lying on top of her and she squirmed against him, tugging at the covers, trying to get them out of the way so that she could get closer to him. As she wrestled with the bedclothes, she felt him go very still.

Suddenly, he lifted his weight off of her and rolled to his back, dragging in great draughts of air as he lay beside her on the bed, pressing his hands against the mattress. His whole body looked like an arrow about to fly from a bowstring, and she knew that was her fault.

"Mack?" she whispered, hearing the broken sound of her own voice.

"We can't do this."

"Why not?" she asked in a shaky voice.

"I came in here because you were having a bad dream. I'm not going to take advantage of you."

"You're not."

"You know damn well I would be!" he said, and the force of his denial shook her to the core.

He was right. She'd reached for him because she was scared, and he'd stopped to give her time to consider what she was doing.

"Thank you," she whispered.

He took another breath and let it out. "Tell me about the dream."

She shuddered. She didn't want to relive it or talk about it. But maybe that was a good way to cool herself down.

"I was back in that horrible funhouse."

"You were Lynn Vaughn again, reliving the experience?"

"No!" Her denial rang out in the darkness of the bedroom.

"Then what?" he asked in the maddeningly reasonable voice she had come to hate.

"I was another woman." She gulped. "His next victim." As she said the last part, her voice broke, and she began to cry.

She tried to scramble off the bed, but Mack reached out, wrapped his fingers around her arm and kept her on the bed. Turning, he cradled her in his arms again. This time there was nothing sexual about the way he held her as he stroked her back and shoulders. It was pure comfort.

She closed her eyes and stayed in his arms, struggling to get control of herself. And finally she was able to shove the tears away as she realized something important. Last time, he'd thought she had some special knowledge of Lynn Vaughn—that she was giving him information she'd gotten in some normal way. Not now.

"This time you'll have to believe me," she whispered, her voice not quite steady.

"What do you mean?"

"It's happening again. But we're together in this hotel suite. You'll have to know I didn't have anything to do with it."

"Okay," he said, but she couldn't help feeling like the response was automatic.

"You'll find out in the morning," she said again.

"Who was it this time?" he asked in flat voice.

She waited a beat, struggling and failing to dredge up a name. "I don't know."

"You said you're always familiar with the person."

"Yes. But this is different. I don't know the woman. At least I don't think so."

"What happened, exactly?"

"It's not all that different from the last time. It's the

same place. Some of the traps are the same. Some are different." She winced.

"What?"

"She was running down a hallway trying to get away and fell through a trapdoor in the floor. When she landed in the basement, I think she broke her arm. She was in a lot of pain, but he was coming after her, so she had to pick herself up and keep going."

She related more details of the dream, wishing she could just wipe the whole thing out of her memory. But that was impossible—and the wrong thing to do. She had to make the man stop, and the only way to do that was to figure out who he was.

"He said he wanted revenge. For ruining his life," she finished.

"But you don't know what the woman did to him?"

"No. And neither did she. She kept asking what she'd done, and he said she knew. But she had no idea."

He nodded, then asked, "Do you know where to find her body?"

"No! Please, don't ask me any more questions."

"Okay."

When he started to shift off the bed, she grabbed his arm. "Will you stay here?"

"And not touch you?" he asked.

"Yes." She swallowed. "Or maybe I'm being too selfish."

"No. I understand."

Did he? She wasn't going to belabor the point. When he settled down beside her, she relaxed a little. After a while, she heard his even breathing, but it was a long time before she could finally fall asleep again.

IN THE MORNING, when her eyes blinked open, it took a moment for her to remember where she was and why

Mack Steele was lying on the bed next to her, shirtless and wearing a pair of jeans.

Then she recalled everything. The kissing. The way she'd rocked against him and cupped his hand over her breast. The way he'd rolled to his back and pressed his palms against the mattress to steady himself.

His eyes were open, and when she looked at his face, she found he was watching her.

"How are you?" he asked.

"Okay."

He looked at the clock, then sat up and reached for the remote that she'd left on the bedside table.

She sat up too, looking down to make sure her legs were covered.

When the television switched on, they were staring at another roadside scene where a male reporter was standing, holding a microphone.

He was saying, "A second woman's body has been found outside of Gaptown. She has been identified as Jeanette Baker."

He went on to give a few more details, but nothing that gave a clue about who had killed her and why.

"Last time they didn't release the name so soon," Jamie murmured.

"I guess two cases put more pressure on them to identify the victim. Do you know her?" Mack asked.

"I told you last night, I don't. And I said that you'd have to believe I wasn't involved, because we were both here when it was happening. Unless you think I climbed out the window and snuck over to the funhouse."

"Of course not!"

"So how did I know, if it wasn't a…psychic dream?"

"I guess there's no other way."

"You guess."

"You want me to confirm that you're having out-of-body experiences?" he snapped, and she knew from his tone that she'd pushed him further than he was willing to go.

She felt tears at the back of her eyes again and clenched her teeth to hold them at bay. Damn, she was in fragile shape. For too many reasons. Before she could start crying in front of Mack again, she climbed out of bed. Keeping her back to him, she rummaged in her overnight bag for clean clothing, then dashed into the bathroom and turned on the shower. Under the spray of the water, she had the feeling that she was shutting out the world.

FROM THE STIFFNESS of Jamie's shoulders when she'd rushed into the bathroom, Mack knew she was upset, and not just by seeing the news account of the murder victim. She'd wanted him to say he believed in her paranormal dreams, but he couldn't get the words out of his mouth, and he wasn't sure why. Maybe it was because of what had happened last night. He'd been pretty close to the edge, but somehow he'd rolled away and stopped himself from making love with her.

He hadn't been lying about the reason for stopping. He didn't want her coming back to him saying that he'd taken advantage of her when she was emotionally vulnerable.

But damn, he wanted her. Not just physically. He wanted to bridge the gap between them emotionally. Which was why he'd told her things about his childhood that he almost always kept private. Unfortunately, he still couldn't deal with the psychic dreams.

He climbed out of bed and ducked out of the room. There was another bathroom in the main part of the suite, and he used it to take a quick shower and dress.

As he shaved, he took a good look at himself, wondering if his background was part of the problem. He hadn't grown up in a normal household. Neither had she, for that matter. Maybe that was why both of them were lousy at communication. It sounded like her mother hadn't known what to say to her about the dreams, and Mrs. Wheeler didn't know what to say to her now about her own life or their relationship. That was something he and Jamie had in common. His own dad had clammed up about his mother. After she'd left, it had been like she had never existed.

Was that normal? Maybe they should have gone to family therapy to work through the pain and anger.

But what was normal, anyway? Maybe everybody was damaged by their backgrounds and secretly as screwed up as he was. Or was he just looking for ways to excuse his fumbling attempts at dealing with his own feelings and Jamie's?

When he stepped into the living room, Jamie had made up the sofa bed for him and was sitting in front of the television with her shoulders slumped, watching another news segment.

He wanted to sit down beside her and pull her into his arms, but he stayed where he was.

She glanced up, then away. "Anything new?" he asked in what he hoped was a neutral voice.

"A guy who knew both Jeanette and Lynn is going to talk to the media."

"His fifteen minutes of fame?"

"I guess."

They sat through commercials for a local grocery store and a national car rental company.

Then one of the station's reporters began talking to a young man with dark hair and a neatly clipped dark beard. He was wearing a corduroy sports jacket and jeans. His name was Aubrey Rollins, and he looked like an upstanding member of the community.

"How did you happen to date both Jeanette and Lynn?" the reporter asked.

Jamie muttered her own question. "And how did they get you on the air so fast? Did you rush down there and volunteer?"

"We were all part of the young men's and women's club at church," he answered the reporter. "They were both wonderful women. Warm and caring." He paused and swallowed. "It was never serious with either one of them, though."

The reporter asked, "And you have no idea who would want to harm them?"

His expression turned thoughtful, and he waited several moments before speaking. "I've been pondering it a lot, and I can't come up with anything. All I can say is that they were really nice women who must have gotten involved in something dangerous."

"Like what?"

He shrugged.

"You think this was something personal with them and they weren't random victims?"

"I guess I was making an assumption." He lifted one shoulder. "You know…because…"

When the interview concluded, Mack muttered, "It could have been him, and he's inserted himself into the limelight."

"People do that?"

"Yeah."

"Doesn't that make it more dangerous for them to avoid getting caught?"

"They think they're smarter than everyone else. Outwitting the authorities is a game with them."

"Yes, the guy with the funhouse called it a game." She

stared at the man on the screen. "He doesn't look like the serial murderer type."

Mack made a snorting sound. "You know how it is when they catch a serial killer. All the neighbors say they can't believe he'd do such a thing."

"Right."

"I'm going to do some research on him."

"Now?"

"No. Let's pack up and go out to breakfast first."

"Pack up?"

"I'd like to switch hotels."

"Why?"

"Change of scenery," he answered.

And then what, he asked himself. He wasn't exactly sure.

Jamie spoke again, interrupting his thoughts. "I don't work every day, but Sabrina's expecting me to come in this morning. I should call her first and let her know I'm okay."

"Sure."

She glanced at her watch, then dug her cell phone out of her purse and called the shop at 43 Light Street. The owner picked up on the second ring.

The transmission was loud enough for Mack to hear both sides of the conversation.

"Jamie, are you all right?" Sabrina asked.

"I'm fine."

She clenched her fingers around the receiver. "I hate to disappear on short notice, but can you manage without me for a few days if I need to be away?"

"Yes. But where are you?"

"Gaptown."

"Are you going to tell me why you're there?"

She looked at Mack, then away. "Something came up."

"About your mom?"

"Partly."

"Okay, I guess you don't want to talk about it. Or tell me why Mack Steele is with you."

She cut him another glance. "You know about that?"

"Come on! This building is like a small town. Word gets around. Everybody knows Mack was on duty at the Light Street Detective Agency when you called the night before last."

Jamie cleared her throat. "As it happens, I'm helping him with an investigation."

"The murders?"

She sucked in a sharp breath. "You know about that?"

"We have TV stations here, too. It's all over the local news." She paused. "I gather you don't want to talk about that, either."

"Not really."

A moment later Jamie clicked off and stood awkwardly in the middle of the room. "You could hear her?"

"Yeah."

"I guess everybody in Baltimore knows we're here together."

He laughed. "No. Just up and down Light Street."

She snorted. "Yeah."

His voice turned sober when he asked, "Does that make you uncomfortable?"

"You know it does."

"We'll make sure everybody understands it's business," he clipped out, wishing it didn't matter so much to Jamie.

"I'm sorry I'm on edge," she said in a small voice.

If he'd felt free to react as he wanted, he would have put

his arms around her. Instead he kept his hands at his sides. "Let's get breakfast. The hotel probably has a buffet."

"I'd rather go out."

"Where?"

She thought for a minute. "There are some fast food restaurants downtown."

After Jamie repacked the clothing and toilet articles she'd taken out, they went downstairs, then back to his car, where they rode in silence until they reached the city center.

"Which way?" he asked.

"Right."

When the tall sign for a familiar chain appeared ahead of them, he turned into the parking lot.

There were no open spots next to the restaurant, so he pulled into a space across the parking area. As soon as he cut the engine, Jamie unbuckled her seat belt and got out.

As she started walking rapidly across the parking lot toward the building, a car shot around the corner.

Mack couldn't see much of the guy behind the wheel because he had a baseball cap pulled down over his face but the car was moving too fast to be in a confined area, and he wanted to yell at the maniac driver to slow down.

He stopped focusing on the driver when he realized that the vehicle was headed straight for Jamie.

Chapter Six

"Watch out," Mack shouted. With no thought for his own safety, he leaped toward Jamie and the speeding car, snatching her out of the way as the vehicle shot past with inches to spare.

Swearing under his breath, he turned her around and held on to her as he craned his neck, watching the vehicle roar out of the parking lot and onto the access road.

When he felt Jamie trembling, he pulled her out of the traffic lane and wrapped his arms around her, holding on tight as he gently rocked her.

"What happened?" she whispered.

"That guy was heading right toward you."

"I…wasn't looking."

"Yeah, you were focused on the restaurant door."

Her head dropped to his shoulder as he stroked her back, holding her protectively against himself, trying to calm the wild beating of his own heart.

That had been damn close. Another couple of inches and the guy would have gotten her.

She could have pulled away, but she stayed in his arms, and he was glad to keep holding her. He wanted to tip her head up so that he could bring her lips to his, but he wasn't going to go that far because the same rules applied as last night. She'd just had a close call, and he'd be taking advantage of her vulnerability.

She moved her head against his shoulder. "Did you see who it was?"

"Unfortunately, no. He had a cap pulled down to hide his face. Do guys usually drive like maniacs in town?"

"I don't know. I guess some do. Like anywhere else."

He kept hanging on to her. "We should go in," he said, although he made no move. "Or do you want to go back to the hotel?"

"We're here now."

"Okay." He looked both ways to make sure someone else didn't have them in his sights. Then he reluctantly eased away.

When she wavered a little on her feet, he slung his arm around her waist and held on to her as they went inside.

They got in line, where they ordered coffee and breakfast sandwiches with eggs and sausage.

When they'd taken their trays to a table by the window, they ate in silence. Finally, he cleared his throat.

As she looked at him inquiringly, he asked the question that had been in his mind since the incident. "How much does Clark Landon dislike you?"

She laughed, but there was no music in the sound. "A lot, I guess. He and I never got along."

"Why?"

"Because he knew I saw he was taking advantage of Mom. But he had the inside track with her, so nothing I had to say about it carried much weight."

Mack took a sip of water. "You got a letter asking you to come home."

She nodded.

"I don't suppose you have it with you."

"It's back in Baltimore. I didn't think I needed it."

Mack nodded. "Could Landon have written it?"

She wiped her lips with her napkin, and he followed the movement. "I don't know. You mean, so he could get me back here and…hurt me?"

"Yeah."

She shrugged. "He's mean, but I never thought of him as homicidal."

"What kind of stuff did he do to you?"

She snorted. "Nothing physical. He made me keep my room super neat. Like he cared! Made me do his stinking laundry. Interrogated any of my friends who were brave enough to come to the house." She shrugged. "I wished I could have afforded my own apartment."

She took another bite of her sandwich.

"The question is, how did he know where we were going to be this morning?" she asked.

Mack looked at her. "I hate to think he could have followed us to the hotel last night and then waited for us and tailed us when we went out."

"There aren't many places to stay in town. He could have come around checking the parking lots."

"Right. Would you call him persistent?"

"He can get focused on something and not let go. Like when a neighbor at his old apartment kept the music on too loud. He complained, and the guy didn't do anything about it. He turned his speakers around so they were facing the wall and blasted the guy. They ended up having a fistfight on the sidewalk."

"How do you know about it?"

"I heard my mom telling a friend."

They finished breakfast, and he scanned the area before he let Jamie walk out of the restaurant.

"I guess it was a good idea to pack before we left. Where are we going now?"

"The library. To do some research. We can find another place to stay later."

Back in the car, she gave him directions to the red-brick colonial-style building across from the Victorian courthouse.

He looked from one to the other. "Eclectic architecture."

"I guess it was the taste of whoever was in charge of the town at the time."

After they parked, Mack brought his laptop inside to one of the tables on the far side of the circulation desk and booted up.

"I can do some checking on my computer," he said.

"On what?"

He lowered his voice. "I've got access to a couple of secure databases where I can research Landon and Aubrey Rollins. Why don't you see what you can find out about Lynn and Jeanette? We can compare notes in an hour."

"Okay."

She went back to the desk and he heard the librarian saying that the system kept twenty years of archives of the local paper, the *Times-News*. They also had the *New York Times,* both on microfiche.

"The reading machine is under the balcony," the woman told her. "Let me show you where to find it."

The two women headed into the stacks.

As Jamie disappeared from view, Mack felt a small pang. Someone had tried to run her over not long ago, and he realized he didn't feel comfortable with her out of his sight. So he moved from the end of the reading room where he'd been sitting to a spot that allowed him to watch her.

She looked around when he sat down nearby. "You don't trust me?"

"I trust you," he answered automatically, then realized he'd stopped thinking she was involved in the murders. He was relieved that she couldn't be. Which left him with the inconvenient conclusion that her knowledge really did come from psychic abilities.

She brought his mind back to the two of them when she asked, "Then why did you follow me over here?"

A woman with wisps of white hair escaping from under a knit cap was looking through books on a nearby shelf. She gave them a dirty look. "This is a library. Kindly keep your voices down," she said in a tart voice.

"Yes, ma'am," Mack answered automatically, then moved closer to Jamie and addressed her in a whisper. "You almost got run over a while ago. I want to make sure you stay safe."

She looked around at the people reading or checking out the material on the shelves. "You think someone would come after me in here?"

"I wasn't expecting trouble in a fast-food parking lot either."

Jamie nodded tightly and sat down at the microfiche reader. She'd used one for college research papers, and she quickly got into the rhythm.

When she glanced over her shoulder, she saw that Mack was studying his computer screen. Feeling a bit guilty, she switched away from the subjects she was supposed to be researching and took a look at something completely different. Something to do with Craig.

She'd met her future husband when he'd first come to Gaptown working an insurance fraud case. Then he'd come back chasing a kidnapper.

She went to the year of the insurance fraud. A quick search didn't turn up anything, probably because the case had hit the papers months after Craig's initial investigation. And she didn't remember exactly when that was.

When she scrolled ahead, she found a story about the kidnapping that had brought him back to town. She wanted to read it right away. Instead she printed it out and went back to the subject she was supposed to be researching: the current murder case.

MACK GLANCED AT JAMIE, then went back to his own research, starting with her mom's boyfriend, Clark Landon, since he could be their most pressing problem. The man hadn't held a steady job in years, apparently, but he'd made bank deposits on a semi-regular basis. Did that mean he had an illegal source of income? Drugs? Maybe up here it was moonshine or stolen freight from the railroad.

Also, as Jamie had already related, the man had been in some minor scrapes with the law. In addition to the fight with the neighbor, he'd been pulled over for DWI a couple of times. And he'd also gotten hauled in after a bar brawl.

Nice guy. The brawl confirmed that Landon had a violent streak, but that didn't mean he'd try to run down Jamie, unless he had a serious anger management problem. Or unless someone had hired him to go after her. Lynn and Jeanette's killer? Did the two men know each other? Assuming the killer was a man. Jamie hadn't seen his face, but her description of the way he operated sounded like he was male.

He made some notes on Landon, then went to the guy who'd dated both Jeanette and Lynn. It turned out that Aubrey Rollins sold real estate for the local office of a national chain. In this climate of declining housing sales, he'd gotten into a dispute with an agent from another company over a commission.

That could indicate that he was either strapped for money or that he was a hard-driving guy determined to get every cent he thought was due him. He was also enterprising. He'd taken advantage of the depressed market to buy a number of cut-rate properties both in town and nearby. Could one of them be the funhouse that Jamie kept talking about?

Mack put the addresses into a file, intending to check on them later.

He was still collecting information when Jamie came back with a stack of papers from the printer, looking like she'd found something interesting.

"What?" he asked.

"You first."

He glanced around and saw that a couple of patrons were watching them with interest.

"Maybe we could go out for a cup of coffee while we talk," he said.

She followed his gaze to their impromptu audience and nodded.

When they stepped outside, she asked, "You really want coffee?"

"No, I just wanted a plausible reason to leave, since we were already attracting attention. We're strangers, and we look like we're doing serious research."

In the car, she asked, "What did you find?"

"Your mom's boyfriend has no steady job."

"I already knew that."

"Apparently he's getting income from somewhere."

She huffed out a breath. "He works for guys who pay in cash."

"Doing what?"

"Some local moving jobs. Some trucking."

"Illegal?"

"Could be."

"He's got some arrests that confirm your assessment of his violent streak."

"That's not news."

Mack drove out of the library lot, checking frequently to see if anyone was behind them. As far as he could tell, nobody was following.

"Did you get a chance to look at Aubrey Rollins?" she asked.

"He sells real estate, and he's taken advantage of the downturn in the market to buy some properties. We'll check them out later."

"Okay, but you got me thinking about coffee."

They drove back downtown and stopped at a coffee shop where they both bought lattes.

When Jamie ordered hers with caramel syrup, he grinned. "You have a sweet tooth."

"Try it. You'll like it."

He did.

When they were back in the car, he asked, "Is there another big hotel chain in town?"

"On Ohio Street."

As they drove, he took in the city. He'd never been in Gaptown before, and he found he liked it. Many of the commercial buildings were from the late nineteenth and early twentieth centuries, which gave the city a charming look.

"This place could be a tourist paradise," he said. "How did I miss it?"

"It's a little off the beaten track, and I'm not sure that making a couple blocks of Baltimore Street into a pedestrian mall was such a great idea."

"It's probably better in summer."

"They need more attractions in the area. You can't keep

a city going on art galleries, restaurants, craft shops and the new hospital complex."

"You've thought about it a lot, I see."

"Of course. Everybody from Gaptown thinks about how to boost the city. One interesting thing—doctors and lawyers from Baltimore and D.C. have bought a lot of the big houses on Washington Street and renovated them. If you want a great old house, you can get one a lot cheaper than in the big city."

She turned from the window back to Mack.

"How long are you planning to stay in town? You're going to run out of hotel chains pretty soon," she observed.

"I don't know. I'd like to have a lead on the guy with the funhouse before we call it quits."

He pulled into the parking lot of another national chain. At the check-in desk, he was able to get another suite. Upstairs, he found that the living room had a small kitchen off the sitting area.

"We can buy stuff for breakfast," he said as he opened cabinets and saw dishes and cutlery.

Jamie lowered herself to the sofa. He pulled out a chair at the small dinette table and sat down facing her.

"Your turn. What did you find out about Jeanette?"

"She was a social worker in Allegany County."

"About the same age as you and Lynn?"

"A couple of years older."

"I wonder how well they knew each other."

"We know they went to the same church."

"Which is?"

"Emmanuel Parish."

"We'll put the ministers on our list."

"As suspects?" she asked in a strained voice.

"I was thinking more of contacts."

She ran her hand over the arm of the sofa, and he wondered what she was thinking. Probably that she didn't like being cooped up in another hotel with Mack Steele. The feeling was mutual, but they were stuck with it for the time being.

She cleared her throat. "I went back through several months of the local papers and found out something else that might fit into the investigation."

When he didn't speak, she went on. "There aren't a lot of murders here, but there was another one a few months ago."

That had him sitting up straighter. "Another woman?"

"No. This was a man. Named Tim Conrad."

"Not necessarily connected."

"But his body was found in the same area where Jeanette and Lynn were dumped."

"Cause of death?"

"I wasn't able to find out."

"Maybe I can get it from the police report."

She glanced at his computer. "You have access to that?"

"Maybe. Did you find out Conrad's occupation?"

"Auto mechanic."

"Okay, let's recap the victims. We have an emergency room nurse, a social worker and an auto mechanic. I wonder what the link is, if any. I guess we can find out if he went to Emmanuel Parish."

"You can do that, too?"

"That one's easy."

He opened the computer, waited for it to resume and checked the church membership list. Tim Conrad wasn't on the roster. Neither was anyone else named Conrad.

"Anything else you can tell me that might connect the three of them?"

"No."

"Maybe if you think about it for a while."

"I have been thinking about it, and there's absolutely nothing more I can tell you."

"You didn't know Conrad?"

"No!" Her voice rose. "And I only knew one of the women." She sat where she was for a few more seconds, gripping the arm of the sofa, then jumped up.

"I need to get out of here."

"Not a good idea."

"Too damn bad. I'm not used to being with anyone for hours on end."

He might have said she spent a lot of time with Sabrina Cassidy at the Light Street Lobby Shop, but he didn't want to say anything to upset her more.

Without looking at him, she strode across the sitting room, pulled open the door and slammed it behind her as she stepped out.

He stared at the door, thinking he shouldn't have pressed her to find a link between the victims. Obviously she was more uncomfortable than he'd thought.

But he couldn't let her go out by herself, not when someone had already tried to run her over.

He made it into the hall in time to see the elevator door close. Damn! It must have been already there when she arrived, and all she had to do was press the button to open the doors.

They were on the fourth floor. Still cursing, he sprinted to the steps, hurtling down and arriving in the lobby as Jamie walked outside.

Before he could follow her, a bellman came in pushing

a cart, blocking Mack's view. When he reached the door, he couldn't see Jamie. Which way had she gone?

He didn't have a clue.

JAMIE HURRIED DOWN THE narrow sidewalk at the edge of the parking lot. There wasn't much place to walk, and she thought maybe she should go back before she got run over. But she wasn't in the mood to go back. Not yet.

She'd thought she could handle the situation with Mack. She'd been okay at the library and in the coffee shop. But in the hotel room, it had suddenly gotten to be too much for her, partly because of Mack's relentless questioning.

But mostly because there was yet another murder that could be connected to the funhouse case. At least if you considered it from the viewpoint of how the bodies had been dumped.

Funhouse case…

She remembered how Craig would come home from the office sometimes and discuss his cases with her. She'd always felt he was asking for her opinion because he wanted another point of view. With Mack, however, she couldn't help feeling like he still thought she was withholding information.

She tried to switch things around and see it from his point of view. What would she think if someone started spouting details of a murder that would be impossible to know, except by psychic means—or by the murderer? She'd done that to him, and of course he'd wondered where she got the information. And if she were honest, she could tell his attitude was shifting. Like he didn't suspect her anymore.

But then why didn't he say so?

And why couldn't she just give him the benefit of the

doubt? Maybe because she felt guilty about getting close to him.

She continued walking along the narrow sidewalk, hardly aware of her surroundings. She kept turning over the details in her mind. He'd gotten them a suite so they didn't have to sleep in the same room. But he'd obviously been keeping an ear out for her, and he'd come to her room last night because she was having another nightmare. They'd ended up pretty close to making love. He was the one who'd pulled away before things went too far. She should be thanking him for that, not be putting the worst possible interpretation on everything he said or did.

She heard a car slow behind her and wondered if Mack had come down the street looking for her.

She expected him to pull up beside her and say, "Get in," in that deep voice of his.

But it wasn't Mack's SUV that drifted up beside her, and the man who got out wasn't Mack. Not unless he was trying to scare her with the ski mask he was wearing.

Coming around the car, the man opened the passenger door and tried to shove her inside.

And she knew in that moment that if he got her into that vehicle, she was going for a one-way ride.

When she started to struggle, he yanked on her upper arm and cursed.

Stiffening her elbows, she pushed against the doorframe, keeping herself out of the front seat as he got behind her and shoved.

"Help! Somebody help!" she shouted.

"Shut up, bitch."

When he socked her between the shoulder blades, she gasped and almost let go of the doorframe, but determination not to let herself be taken kept her fighting. He took one hand off her and fumbled with something she couldn't see. A gun?

"Help!" she shouted again, praying that someone would come along the street.

Because she was losing the battle. Sooner or later he would get her into the vehicle.

Chapter Seven

Mack had exited the hotel and taken several steps to the left when he heard a woman shout, "Help! Somebody help me!"

The cry sounded like Jamie, and it came from behind him. On a curse, he reversed direction and started running, hearing another voice.

It was a man, shouting, "Shut up."

His heart leaped into his throat as he scanned the parking lot. Jamie wasn't there. But he spotted her on the sidewalk, struggling with a man beside an SUV.

When he saw that the guy was trying to force her into the passenger seat, his insides clenched. She was putting up a pretty good fight, but the guy was taller and heavier, and eventually he was going to win.

Although Mack's gun was in a back holster, he couldn't risk a shot, not when the man was in close contact with Jamie.

But he'd been a pitcher on his baseball team in high school. Along the edge of the parking lot were decorative rectangles full of rounded rocks in place of flower beds. Scooping up some of the rocks, he wound up like he was on the pitcher's mound and let the first missile fly. Then he let loose with another. The rocks hit the side of the SUV next to the guy, who stopped what he was doing and whirled to stare back at Mack. It was then that Mack saw the ski mask that effectively hid the would-be kidnapper's features.

"Get the hell off of her," Mack shouted as he ran forward, pulling his weapon and putting on a burst of speed.

The abductor hesitated for a moment, then must have decided to cut his losses. He threw Jamie to the pavement, dashed around his vehicle and climbed back into the driver's seat. Before Mack could reach the SUV, the vehicle was already roaring away.

Mack's eyes shot to the license plate, but the guy wasn't taking any chances on being identified that way. The plate was smeared with mud, hiding the numbers and letters. About all Mack could tell was that it looked like the standard Maryland variety, not one of the fancy "Save the Bay" models.

He ran to Jamie, holstering his weapon and coming down on the ground beside her.

"Are you all right?" he asked urgently as he scanned her face and body. Her hair was messed up and she was breathing hard, but he didn't see blood anywhere.

"Yes," she gasped out.

"What happened?"

She craned her neck to stare down the street, but the SUV was already out of sight.

"I was walking down the sidewalk, and he pulled up beside me and tried to shove me into his car." She swallowed. "I couldn't see his face. He was wearing a ski mask."

"Yeah. I saw. Did he try to hurt you?"

"He socked me in the back when he couldn't get me into the vehicle."

Mack nodded. "His license plate was covered with mud." He waited for a moment. "Can you get up?"

She kept her face away from him. "I think so."

He wanted to pull her into his arms, but getting her inside was more important. He stood, then reached for her hand and helped her to her feet. With her head down, she kept a tight hold on his hand, and when she wavered a little, he steadied her with an arm around her waist. He might have told her that she shouldn't have gone out, but he didn't think that would do either one of them any good, so he kept his mouth shut.

"Can you walk?"

"Of course!" she answered in a sharp voice, then sighed. "Sorry, I didn't mean to snap at you."

"We're fine," he answered automatically, wondering what that meant, exactly. They certainly hadn't been fine when she'd fled the hotel. And her recent brush with disaster couldn't have made things better.

As they started back toward the building, her gait quickened and steadied, but when he saw that she had her bottom lip between her teeth, he knew she was struggling to hold herself together.

They reached the lobby and people looked up the way they often did when somebody new entered the scene. Trying to ignore the stares, he kept his arm around Jamie as they waited for the elevator. Once inside, she closed her eyes, leaning her head and shoulders against the wall.

When they reached the fourth floor, she rushed down the hall. He hurried to follow, his key card in his hand so he could unlock the door and let her in.

She stopped in the hallway to the living room, keeping her head down. When he tipped her chin up, he saw tears glistening in her eyes.

"It's all right to cry," he murmured.

"I feel like such a jerk."

"Why?"

"I know damn well I shouldn't have gone outside when I was too upset to pay attention to my surroundings."

He could only nod, then pull her close. She held herself stiffly for a moment, then relaxed against him, and he rocked her in his arms, silently thanking God that the guy hadn't shoved her into the car. Because he had the awful feeling that he never would have seen her again. Not alive, anyway.

"Thank you for saving me," she whispered.

"You were fighting him. You held him off long enough for me to get there."

"He was trying to get something."

"What?"

"I don't know. A gun, maybe." She hesitated a second. "Did you throw rocks at him?"

"Yeah, I couldn't risk a shot."

She nodded against his shoulder and whispered, "Clever."

"You don't know who it was?"

"No idea."

"Clark Landon?"

"It might have been."

"I'm going to have a chat with him."

Her fingers dug into his shoulders. "Don't leave me."

"Of course not," he answered, caught between warring emotions. He was still trying to come to grips with what had almost happened, and at the same time he was elated that she wanted him with her. Or was it just that she was afraid to be alone after two frightening incidents? First in the parking lot of the fast-food restaurant and now at the hotel?

He didn't know, couldn't ask. Yet when she raised her

face trustingly to him, he couldn't stop himself from lowering his head. The touch of his mouth to hers was like an emotional explosion that he couldn't control. And maybe it was the same for her, because her lips moved urgently under his. When she opened for him, he accepted the invitation, and his tongue played with the insides of her lips, her teeth, and then deeper.

She murmured his name, holding him more tightly, and he knew that he was on the verge of losing control.

"Jamie?"

"Don't go away," she said again.

"Never," he whispered, his hands stroking her shoulders, down her back, up her spine, then back down again to cup her bottom. When she didn't resist, he pulled her more tightly against himself, his breath catching as he pressed her to the erection straining at the front of his jeans. He went still, waiting for her to pull away, but she stayed where she was, and he couldn't summon the will to stop.

"Jamie," he said again, hearing the desperation in his own voice.

Last night he'd vowed not to take advantage of her when she was emotionally vulnerable. Was he doing that now? He hoped not, because he couldn't deal with the loss if he had to turn her loose.

She made small, broken sounds as he rocked her in his arms, sounds that sent the blood racing through his veins.

Still he made no move to leave the hallway until he heard her say, "Come into the bedroom."

The invitation made his heart beat faster. And faster still when her hands began to move restlessly across his back, then down to the waistband of his jeans. With her arms around him she pulled his shirt from the back of his pants, then slipped her hand under, pressing her palm against the naked skin of his back, sliding fingers over his warm flesh, sending shivers over his skin.

He closed his eyes, marveling at the way her touch made him feel hot and cold at the same time. And marveling at the wonderful taste of her as she continued to kiss him.

When he realized they were still standing in the hallway, he knit his fingers with hers and led her into the bedroom, moving slowly, still giving her the chance to stop if she changed her mind. He wanted her badly, but he would hold back if it wasn't right for her.

They stepped into the bedroom together, and he turned to kiss her again, silently admitting his greed.

As she had done a few moments earlier, he pulled her shirt out of her waistband and slipped his hands underneath, reveling in the way the silky skin of her back felt under his trembling fingers. Unable to deny himself, he brought his mouth back to hers for frantic kisses that left him breathless.

Her hands were at the front of his shirt now, undoing the buttons, then pushing the sides apart so that she could slide her hands over his chest. He sighed as her fingers tangled in his thick hair, then found his nipples and flicked back and forth across them.

It seemed like a miracle that she was in his arms, touching him so intimately. Maybe later they would have second thoughts, but at this moment there was no room for doubt between them.

Stepping away from her, he drew the drapes across the window, then turned on the bathroom light and closed the door most of the way so that there was enough illumination to see her but not too much to break the spell.

He was dizzy with desire for her. Desperate to feel her breasts against his chest, he yanked his arms out of his sleeves and tossed the shirt on the floor. Then he worked the buttons of her shirt, sliding it off her shoulders. Before he could stop himself, he reached around her and unhooked her bra, pulled it away from her and dropped it on the floor, along with the shirt.

"Lord, you are so beautiful," he whispered as his gaze swept over her gentle curves. Unable to hold back, he gathered her into his arms, a sound of gratitude rising in his throat as he absorbed the feel of her against himself.

It was difficult to draw in a full breath, difficult to keep his balance as he swayed her in his arms so that her breasts moved back and forth against his body.

She moaned as her nipples slid against the rough hair on his chest.

He fumbled with the snap at the top of her jeans, opening it and lowering the zipper so that he could drag the pants down her legs along with her panties. She kicked them away and stood naked in his arms.

It felt wonderful to slide his hands over the curve of her bottom, her hips, the indentation at her waist, all the places he'd longed to touch. Imagined touching.

Easing a little away, he managed to get his belt buckle undone, then his zipper. But he kept his briefs on as he kicked his jeans away.

He had imagined this so many times. Yet the reality was so much better than any daydream, and he marveled at the intensity of what he felt now.

Turning to the side, he bent to pull the covers back, then brought her down to the bed with him, rolling to his side, holding her in his arms.

His gaze on her face, he cupped her breasts, shaping them to his touch, then played his thumbs over her distended nipples.

She closed her eyes, her breath catching as he bent to

take one hard peak into his mouth, drawing on her as he used his thumb and finger on the other side.

"Oh, Mack," she cried out.

Gratified by her response, he slid one hand down her body, into her hot, moist folds. He had never needed a woman more, yet he wasn't going to rush this. Not when he sensed the moment was so important.

He touched her and kissed her, tasted her, lifting his head to watch her face and judge her readiness as he continued to stroke her most intimate flesh.

He saw passion color her features, felt her hips lift restlessly against his fingers.

"Look at me," he asked as he pulled off his briefs, then moved over her, parting her legs with his knee.

Her eyes met his, and everything inside him clenched.

When his body sank into hers, he felt as though it was a homecoming.

Lifting his head, he stared down at her, overcome with emotions he couldn't name as he began to move inside her. He had wanted her for a long time, and finally she was his.

She threw back her head on the pillow while she matched his rhythm. Her fingers dug into his shoulders as she climbed toward orgasm with him. Summoning every ounce of self-control he possessed, he held himself back, waiting for her to reach the peak of her pleasure. When he felt her body start to contract around him, he let go, crying out as climax rocketed through him.

As the storm passed, he looked down at her. For a moment, he saw a look of wonder in her eyes, and he thought that she was finally ready to admit that they belonged together. Then she must have realized she was with

Mack Steele. As she stared at him, she took her lower lip between her teeth.

"Jamie?"

When she didn't answer, he shifted his weight off of her, coming down beside her on the bed.

"We shouldn't have done that," she whispered.

"Don't tell me it was wrong," he managed to say around the lump that had formed in his throat.

"It was."

"Give me a good reason why."

She didn't answer, and he wondered if she could come up with anything logical or if she was just clinging to old assumptions.

Fumbling for her hand, he clasped his fingers with hers. Was there anything he could say to convince her that she was a free woman? That the two of them were right for each other, and no memory of the past should come between them?

When she started to move away, he held on to her.

"Stay with me. I need you."

"Why?"

It was hard to get the words out, but he managed to say, "Because making love with you was the best thing that's happened to me in a long time, and I don't want you to tell me it was wrong."

"It was."

"No. And I'd like a chance to prove that to you."

"How?"

He wanted to say that he'd make love with her all over again, and it would be just as good. But great sex wasn't the answer to his problem. He wanted the two of them to merge their lives. He wanted her to realize how amazing they were together. Not just in bed.

And most of all he wanted to tell her he was in love

with her, but he didn't think she wanted to hear that piece of information. "Just give me a chance," he said in a low voice.

She dragged in a breath and let it out. "Maybe I can't."

"Well, I'm not going to force you into anything," he said, waiting for her to tell him that he just had. It wouldn't be true. But if she thought so, he had no defense.

Long seconds passed, and when she didn't say anything, he felt a tiny bit of the tension ease out of him.

"We should talk about the man and the SUV," he said, because he needed to change the subject.

"Okay. But not in here."

She pulled the spread around her as she climbed out of bed and began collecting her clothes.

He lay where he was until she disappeared into the bathroom. Then he quickly jumped out of bed and gathered up his own clothing. He climbed into his pants before straightening the sheet and blanket. Then he stepped into the sitting room to put on the rest of his clothing.

IF STAYING IN THE BATHROOM all day was an option, Jamie might have taken that route. But she had to be honest with herself. One reason she was upset was that making love with Mack had been wonderful. He was a skilled lover and a considerate one, and she'd been without a man for so long. She wanted that to be the reason the fireworks had exploded between them, but she wouldn't—couldn't—lie to herself. There was something between them. Something she was sure that a normal woman would want to explore.

Did that mean she wasn't normal?

Unable to come to any conclusions, she took a quick shower, then dried her hair. She didn't bother with makeup as she stepped back into the bedroom. Mack had pulled up the sheet and smoothed it out. She finished the job by tugging the spread back into place, making it look like nobody had been making love there.

Then she walked into the living room where Mack was sitting with his gaze trained on the television.

He could have asked how she was feeling. He could have said a dozen different things. When he remained silent, she took the seat at the other end of the couch where she'd have to turn her head if she wanted to look at him. When he used the remote to snap off the TV, she jumped.

He gestured toward the coffeemaker in the kitchen area. "Do you want some coffee?"

"I'm fine."

"So what can you tell me about the guy who tried to push you into the SUV?" he said, as though the time they'd spent in bed together hadn't really happened.

She focused on the incident. The one that had sent her burrowing into Mack's arms. "I already told you he was wearing a ski mask, so I couldn't see his face."

"I believe you can tell me more than you think. What color were his eyes?"

She allowed his face to jump back into her vision and winced. "Are you okay?" Mack asked quickly.

"Yes. I was just thinking about him grabbing me. Then struggling with him." She swallowed. "His eyes were brown."

"Okay. Good."

"That's not much."

"Did he have a big head? A small one?"

"About average."

"Big nose? I mean, did it make the front of the ski mask poke out?"

"Yes. But I'm not sure it was super big."

"What about his hands?"

She hadn't realized he could get so much out of her, but the question brought back another detail. "His nails were neatly cut and clean."

"Okay. So that means he's probably not an auto mechanic or anything that involves manual labor."

"And his hands were fairly large."

"Another good detail."

"But not enough to figure out who he is."

"What was he wearing?"

Again, she pictured the incident, and details came back to her. "Jeans. Scuffed boots. A casual jacket. Nothing we can take to the police."

"The SUV was black."

"Yes. And… I remember the interior was beige," she added as another tidbit surfaced.

"Was the interior neat or messy?"

"Neat. I didn't see anything lying around except…" She stopped short and winced.

"What?"

"I saw a pair of handcuffs. Obviously for me." The last part came out high and breathless.

"Anything else you can tell me?"

She thought for a few minutes and shook her head. "Oh, wait. I think I scratched his neck with my nails."

"Okay. That might help, if we find him." He paused for a moment. "Let's go back to Clark Landon. Could it have been him?"

"He was about the right size but I don't think Clark has that vehicle. Nor would his car be so clean and neat."

He answered with a harsh laugh. "He could have stolen it, for all we know."

They sat in silence for a few more minutes. Finally,

Jamie moved restlessly on the couch. "Maybe I should get some rest."

"You should eat something."

"Like what?"

Mack got up and walked to the desk, where he picked up a menu. "There's a restaurant right in the hotel. I can bring us back something."

"Okay," she answered without enthusiasm. She wasn't really hungry, but it would be a bad idea to make a habit of missing meals.

He handed her the menu, and she scanned the selections. "Hamburger and fries, I guess."

He dialed the number and ordered two hamburgers and two orders of fries, then said he'd pick up the food.

When he left the suite, she got up and walked back to the bathroom, where she used her brush and the dryer to straighten out her hair. Maybe she did care…a little.

Mack was back with the meal they'd ordered in a few minutes. "What's that for?" she asked when she saw two chocolate milkshakes.

"For fun."

"Fun. Yeah."

They started eating in silence. She didn't know if the burgers were good or bad. She was just eating to keep herself going. But she did like the chocolate shake, she silently admitted.

Probably because they were both uncomfortable, he turned on the TV and they watched the news again. The local stations were still talking about the murders, but they didn't have any new information.

When he suddenly said, "Maybe it's time for you to go back to Baltimore," her head snapped up.

"You wanted me to come along. What's changed?"

"That's not exactly the way I remember it."

Chapter Eight

"Whatever you remember, I'm not going back," Jamie said, punching out the words.

Mack had an answer ready. "It's the safest thing for you."

"Why?"

He set down the burger he was eating and spread his hands. "Because you've been attacked twice now. Someone tried to run you down in a parking lot. Then they tried to kidnap you. Those incidents must be related either to the funhouse investigation or to Clark Landon. Neither alternative is good."

She felt her expression turn defiant. "Maybe, but I'm not leaving. I want to see this through."

"Even if you get killed," he snapped.

"Are you trying to frighten me?"

"Maybe I'm trying to make you think logically."

She could feel her jaw hardening as she spoke. "It's not that far to home, and my address is in the same database where you looked up Lynn Vaughn. If someone is after me in Gaptown, they could follow me back home. Maybe I'm safer with you than I would be in my own house."

A satisfied expression flashed across his face so quickly that she wasn't sure she'd actually seen it. Did he really want her to go home, or was he glad she was insisting on staying with him?

"Let's go on the assumption that the sooner we solve the murders, the better," she said.

"You think we can?"

"That's why we're hanging around, isn't it?"

"Yeah."

"Then why don't we talk to Tim Conrad's wife," she heard herself say.

He looked at his watch. "I guess it's not too late for a business call. Okay. Let's."

"You know where she lives?"

"I looked up the address after you found his name."

They finished their meal quickly.

She saw Mack's watchful expression as they headed for the elevator. He was even more vigilant when they reached the lobby.

"You wait here. I'm going to get the car."

She could have objected. Instead she said, "All right."

The lobby was almost empty, and she kept her eyes on the people there: a couple of female desk clerks, a businessman checking in and an older couple with luggage who must have been waiting for an airport shuttle or something. As she studied the people, she suddenly wondered if the clerks knew anything.

Walking to the counter, she waited until a man checking in had wheeled his suitcase to the elevator. Then she said, "My name is Jamie Shepherd. Did anyone come in or call about my staying here?"

"Not that I know of," the clerk answered. "But I've only been on duty a couple of hours."

"Thanks."

Mack had pulled close to the door, and she hurried to join him, surprised at her sudden feeling of exposure as she stepped outside. It didn't feel good to know that someone might be watching her. She scanned the area but didn't see anyone obviously paying attention to them. Still, she kept looking around as they drove out of the parking lot and onto the highway.

"What did you say to the desk clerk?" he asked.

"I wanted to know if anyone had inquired about me."

"Did they?"

"Not as far as the woman knew, but she'd only been on duty for a few hours."

"Or she could have been paid not to say anything."

"Oh, thanks."

He glanced toward her, then in the rearview mirror. "Just being realistic. Maybe we should have registered under false names. Too bad I wasn't thinking we needed to hide our identities."

She answered with a tight nod, then folded her arms across her chest.

Mack kept checking in the rearview mirror and watching any cars that pulled beside them.

"Do you see anyone suspicious?" she asked.

"No. And I'm hoping not to."

They exited the highway and headed toward Tim Conrad's house. It was in a working class neighborhood where a lot of the houses needed painting and the driveways held more pickups than cars. The Conrad house was a small rancher with dull white siding and window trim. As she looked at it, Jamie felt her stomach knot. She had been depressed and worried about her future for a long time after Craig had died. The woman who lived here could be in similar shape.

"Do we just knock on the door?" Jamie asked.

"Yes."

"And what do we say?"

"I was thinking about that on the way over. Probably our best bet is to just say we're investigating homicides in the area."

"For whom?"

"The Light Street Detective Agency."

There was a low hedge around the front yard. Beyond it, the sidewalk was cracked. And the front porch had settled so that the structure leaned forward slightly.

When they knocked at the door, there was no answer for several moments. Then a boy of about ten lifted the blinds in one of the front windows and looked at them.

"What do you want?" he called through the window.

"We'd like to talk to your mom. Is she home?"

He went away, and Jamie wasn't sure if he was coming back. Then the front door opened, and a thin, blond woman who appeared to be in her early thirties looked at them inquiringly.

"Sorry to bother you, Mrs. Conrad. We're from the Light Street Detective Agency in Baltimore," Mack said, getting out his credentials and showing them to her.

"And?"

"We're investigating murders that have occurred in Gaptown during the past year."

The woman gave a little nod. "I'm not sure how I can help you."

"Can we come in? I'd like to ask you a few questions about your husband."

Her expression was resigned as she stepped aside, and they walked into a small, cluttered living room. On a chest at one side of the room were some framed photos. Jamie saw a picture of the boy, his mother and the man who must have been his father. Like his wife, Tim Conrad appeared to be in his early thirties. He wasn't much taller than his wife, and his light-brown hair was cut short. In the picture, he was smiling.

Jamie looked away, thinking that Mrs. Conrad kept the reminder of happier times in full view. Jamie had done the opposite and put her pictures of Craig away.

The boy was sitting on the floor in front of an old television set with one of the boxes that converted the signal to digital. He seemed to be ignoring them, yet Jamie had the feeling he was taking everything in.

His mother must have had the same thought because she said, "Tommy, you go on to your room."

The boy got up slowly and left.

Mrs. Conrad gestured toward the couch. "I guess you might as well sit down."

"Thank you," they both said.

As she sat down, Jamie wondered what it would be like to have a son to take care of on her own.

"I'm sorry about your husband," she said.

The woman nodded.

"Are you getting along okay?"

"I had some insurance. And I'm an aide at West Side Elementary School. So we're getting by."

"I know it's hard," Jamie murmured. She had had insurance, too. Quite a lot, actually, because the Light Street Detective Agency had a very generous policy for employees. But financial security didn't make up for the loss of a spouse.

The woman's expression turned fierce. "How would you know?"

Jamie clenched her hands in her lap as she answered. "My husband was killed last year."

Mrs. Conrad's expression softened. "Oh, I'm sorry. I shouldn't have jumped on you like that."

"Sometimes it's hard to keep your perspective." Jamie

glanced quickly at Mack. He was watching them, and she figured he'd decided she was the best person to get information out of Mrs. Conrad. She hated to use that connection, yet she understood its effectiveness.

"What happened to your husband?" the other woman asked.

"Hit and run accident."

"Oh. That must have been rough on you."

"No worse than what you went through," Jamie answered. She dragged in a breath and let it out. "Did the police come up with any clues about what happened to Tim?"

"Nothing. They assumed it was a robbery gone wrong."

"He was an auto mechanic?"

"Yes."

"And the body shop was robbed?"

"Yes." Mrs. Conrad shifted in her seat. "You said you were investigating murders." She glanced toward the hallway where her son had disappeared, then lowered her voice. "Does this have anything to do with those two women who were killed recently?"

"We think it may."

"Why?"

She glanced at Mack, wondering how much was okay to say.

He answered, "Because your husband was found in the same area."

"Oh. I didn't realize."

"Did you or your husband know either of the women who were recently murdered?" she asked.

"Tell me their names again."

"Lynn Vaughn and Jeanette Baker."

Mrs. Conrad thought for a few moments, then shook

Send For
2 FREE BOOKS
Today!

I accept your offer!

Please send me two
free Harlequin Intrigue®
novels and two mystery
gifts (gifts worth about $10).
I understand that these books
are completely free—even
the shipping and handling will
be paid—and I am under no
obligation to purchase anything, ever,
as explained on the back of this card.

**About how many NEW paperback fiction books have you
purchased in the past 3 months?**

❏ 0-2	❏ 3-6	❏ 7 or more
E9KY	**E9LC**	**E9LN**

❏ I prefer the regular-print edition
182/382 HDL

❏ I prefer the larger-print edition
199/399 HDL

Please Print

FIRST NAME

LAST NAME

ADDRESS

APT.#   CITY

STATE/PROV.   ZIP/POSTAL CODE

Visit us online at
www.ReaderService.com

Offer limited to one per household and not applicable to series that subscriber is currently receiving.

Your Privacy—The Reader Service is committed to protecting your privacy. Our Privacy Policy is available online at www.ReaderService.com or upon request from the Reader Service. We make a portion of our mailing list available to reputable third parties that offer products we believe may interest you. If you prefer that we not exchange your name with third parties, or if you wish to clarify or modify your communication preferences, please visit us at www.ReaderService.com/consumerschoice or write to us at Reader Service Preference Service, P.O. Box 9062, Buffalo, NY 14269. Include your complete name and address.

© 2010 HARLEQUIN ENTERPRISES LIMITED. ® and ™ are trademarks owned and used by the trademark owner and/or its licensee. Printed in the U.S.A. ▶ Detach card and mail today. No stamp needed. ▶ H-I-01/11

her head. "I'm sorry. I never heard those names before. Obviously they didn't stick in my mind from the news accounts."

"Can you think of anything that would link your husband to them?"

"Like what?"

"Anything at all."

She gave a small shrug. "They all lived in Gaptown, I guess."

"Yeah," Mack said, jumping into the conversation. "You never went to the Emmanuel Parish Church?"

She shook her head. "We're Baptists. That's Episcopalian."

Mack asked another question. "Did anything unusual happen to your husband in the days or weeks before he was killed?"

"Unusual like what?"

"Did he come home and tell you he'd had a fight with a customer? Did he have any disputes about money?"

Again, she considered the question. "Of course people would get mad at him when the police called and asked him to tow their cars. They'd act like it was his fault."

"Right. Any incident in particular?"

"I can't think of anything."

"Was he having any disputes with his friends or relatives?"

"No. Tim was a very…mild-mannered guy. He did his job, but he wasn't really good friends with any of the men at the shop. Getting into fights with people wasn't his style."

Mack nodded and stood. "We appreciate your talking to us. Thank you so much for your time. If you think of anything, please let us know." He took out his wallet, pulled out a card, and handed it to her.

She looked at it, then bent it back and forth in her hand, and Jamie wondered if she was going to toss it into the trash when they left.

"We're going to be in town for a few days," he added. "If you want to talk to us in person again, let me know. We'll be glad to come back over."

When they exited the house, Jamie dragged in a breath and let it out in a rush.

"She's got it tough."

"I guess it was hard for you to talk to her."

"Yes. But I wanted to do it."

As she started toward the car, he held his arm in front of her. "Wait a minute."

Once again, he scanned the area before dropping his arm. "Okay. Come on."

When he started for the car, she hurried to keep up. They both got in, and he locked the door.

Mack waited until he'd driven off before saying, "What she says doesn't make perfect sense."

"What do you mean?"

"She said there was a robbery at the auto shop where he worked. Then he turned up dead along the road."

"So?"

"If someone killed him and stayed around long enough to rob the auto shop, you'd think they'd want to get out of there quickly when they were finished, but they took the time to wrap him up in a tarp and bundle him into their car. That was taking an additional risk."

"What are you suggesting?"

"Maybe someone wanted it to look like a robbery, but there was actually another motive. Maybe they didn't even kill him there. He could have been in the funhouse like the other victims, only nobody knew about it. Nobody knows about it now but us."

"Because of my dreams," she murmured.

"Yeah."

She felt a small jolt of satisfaction. So he believed in the dreams. But she didn't press him on it. "How do we find out?" she asked instead.

"Keep digging. If the three murders are connected, we'll come up with something."

"We've already been digging for a couple of days."

"This isn't a TV show where the detective has to solve the crime in an hour minus commercials." He stopped a moment and then muttered under his breath, "We should have asked her more about the towing he did for the police department."

"Why would that be significant?"

"Because the murders could have something to do with a police case." He turned the corner, checking his mirrors. "We can probably check on that online."

"You think that's true of the women, too?"

"I don't know."

She sat quietly for a few moments, then changed topics. "If it was the killer who went after me, how would he even know who I am?"

"He could have been lurking around the site where Lynn Vaughn was dumped."

"Why would he do that? Wouldn't that be dangerous for him?"

"Some unsubs like to get involved."

"Unsubs?"

"Unknown subjects. If you don't know his name, it's a convenient designation. He could even have tipped the cops off on where to find the body, then made sure he had a hiding place where he could watch. He might even have picked the location with that in mind."

"But why?"

"Because it added to his satisfaction to watch the cops discover the body."

She shivered.

"We're talking about someone who's…disturbed. Or very focused on this set of circumstances."

"And you're saying he saw us? But why did he go after me and not you?"

"If you had to make a choice, would you go after a six-foot, two-hundred-pound guy or a five-foot-four, hundred-pound woman?"

"You have a point. But I weigh more than that."

"Not much."

"There's something else," she said. "The women were dumped beside the road, with no attempt to make it look like anything but murder. But Mrs. Conrad said the station actually was robbed. That sounds different."

"That could be right. Or the guy could have decided that once he got away with the first one, he didn't need to fake anything."

MACK SLID JAMIE A sideways glance. He liked the way she was thinking this through, coming up with ideas. And he liked the way she'd dealt with Mrs. Conrad. She was good with people, and she had the advantage of sharing a very personal experience with the woman. He'd watched them together, and he was sure that the bond of widow-hood had helped in the interview. As far as he could see, the woman was being straight with them. She'd told them what she knew, which wasn't much. But she had his card, and maybe she'd think of something later.

They stopped at a grocery store on the way back and got some supplies, including milk, cereal and bags of chips and pretzels.

Jamie sighed as they brought the bags to the suite. "I hate living on this stuff."

"You'd rather cook?" he asked.

"Actually, I would."

"If you could fix anything you wanted, what would it be?" he asked as he set down the food on the dinette table.

She thought for a moment. "Coq au vin."

"Fancy!"

She grinned. "Just a French name for chicken in wine sauce."

"I'd love to taste it."

The grin faded from her face, and he thought he'd stepped over another line that she didn't want him to cross. First he'd made love to her. Now he was thinking about her cooking for him.

Slow down, Steele, he warned himself.

When Jamie excused herself and disappeared into her room, he breathed out a little sigh. He had some business to attend to, and he'd like to slip out while she was sleeping.

That sounded like a good plan until he remembered that she might have a nightmare, and he wouldn't be there to wake her up and hold her in his arms.

Was that what he wanted? Any excuse to climb into her bed again?

He wrote her a message on the hotel notepad, telling her he was going out, and if she woke up, she should stay in the suite. He set it on the sofa where he assumed she'd see it if she came into the living room. Still, he didn't like leaving her.

Before he could change his mind, he stepped into the hall, closing the door quietly behind himself.

IN THE BEDROOM, JAMIE lay rigidly in bed. When she heard the door close, she waited for several moments, then got up and cautiously opened the bedroom door. Mack was not in the living room, and when she walked in and looked around she found a note on one of the sofa cushions.

I have to go out for a little while. Don't leave the suite while I'm away. Mack.

Now he was giving her orders. And not even telling her where he was going.

Damn!

A while ago, she'd thought about making him dinner—which was not a good sign. She was a good cook, and she'd made dinners for Craig to impress him before they were engaged. She didn't have to make an impression on Mack Steele. They weren't dating.

No, she'd skipped that step and gone right to bed with him.

She clenched and unclenched her fists. She should call one of her friends who was still in town and ask if they could drive her back to Baltimore. In the next second, she remembered that she'd insisted on staying here to help with the investigation.

She couldn't even keep her priorities straight. What did she want more—to find the killer or to get away from Mack? Maybe she should leave *him* a note saying that she was getting her own room. Only he'd told her not to go out. And come to think of it, the killer had tracked them down here once. He could come back.

Her gaze shot to the door. Quickly she crossed the room and pushed the safety bar into place, making it impossible for anyone to open the door from the outside. Now she'd have to wait up for Mack to let him back in, and she would have preferred to be in her room when he came home. On the other hand, she wanted to ask where he'd sneaked off to. Or was that acting like a wife who didn't trust her husband?

No. Not at all. It didn't matter to her if he was seeing another woman, although that was hardly likely in Gaptown. He didn't know anyone here.

She stopped short in the middle of the room and ran a shaky hand through her hair, knowing that her thoughts were completely jumbled. She should be focused on finding out who had killed those three people, and instead she was worrying about her relationship with Mack. She could no longer deny she was falling for him. Still, she didn't have to go racing into his arms.

Walking to the desk, she pulled open a drawer and found the local phone book. If Mack wasn't going to take her out to investigate the case, she could do something here. She still knew plenty of people in town. Maybe someone could give her information about Aubrey Rollins, the guy who'd dated both women. Maybe by the time Mack got back, she could tell him something he didn't know.

Flipping through the book, she thought of old friends, then settled on Marilyn Westerly and dialed her number. They'd been friends in high school, and Marilyn had come to her wedding in Baltimore.

Her wedding… she pushed that out of her mind and began to dial.

MACK TURNED ONTO THE street where Jamie's mom lived, then drove past the house, looking at the lights in the front window and the beat-up Ford parked in front. He remembered seeing it when they'd first come over. Then Clark Landon had gone out, and the car had no longer been there. It must be his.

Of course, it wasn't the truck that had tried to run Jamie

over. Or the SUV from this afternoon. But it was easy enough to borrow—or steal—another vehicle.

So was Landon home or not? And if so, how long would he stay home?

Mack wanted to talk to the guy, but he didn't want Jamie's mother to know about it, so he drove to the end of the block, then pulled up under a maple tree and sat watching the house.

Twenty minutes later, Clark Landon strolled outside and walked to his vehicle. Mack slapped the steering wheel and uttered, "All right."

Maybe the guy was going to a place he'd rented out in the country and had turned into a funhouse. Or maybe he was just getting away from the woman of the house, since she didn't seem like the kind of person you'd want to hang around with and make happy conversation.

When Landon drove away, Mack hung back, then started his SUV and waited until the guy was almost to the corner before following. He drove toward downtown, then veered off into a commercial area, where he pulled into a parking lot beside a bar called Louie's. The lot was full of pickup trucks and SUVs.

From across the street, Mack studied the grimy red brick exterior of the one-story building with a neon sign in the front window that said, "Open." He remembering that Landon had mentioned the place when he'd left the house the night before.

Mack drove a little way down the block and parked, waiting in his car until Landon went inside, then gave the man another ten minutes to get settled in his regular routine before crossing the street.

When Mack stepped inside, the smell of beer and smoke almost knocked him over. He let the door close behind him and stood there looking around. The walls were made of old-style knotty pine paneling, and peanut shells littered the floor. The tables were old and wooden, with barrel-shaped chairs around them. The bar was nothing special and occupied the wall across from the door. Behind it were several lighted signs advertising beer companies.

It was a working man's establishment. All the patrons were men, and all were dressed in jeans and flannel shirts or work shirts—Landon included. He was standing at the end of the bar with a mug of beer in his hand.

Mack studied the man. He was almost six feet tall and a bit on the chunky side. With the ski mask, he could be the guy who'd tried to force Jamie into the SUV, but there was no way of knowing for sure. Were his eyes brown?

Mack walked up beside Landon and slid onto a bar stool, like he was just a regular coming in for a drink.

Landon didn't look to see who was beside him. Did he usually like to drink alone, Mack wondered, or was something eating at him?

The bartender came over, looking him up and down, probably wondering how the stranger had found his way into this place.

"What'll you have?"

"Wild Duck," Mack answered.

At the sound of his voice, the man he'd been following turned his head, looking surprised.

"You!"

Mack answered with a tiny nod.

"What are you doing here?"

"I'm thirsty."

"There are plenty of other places to drink in town."

Mack shrugged. When his beer arrived, he took a sip.

"What do you really want?" Landon asked.

"To make you think."

"What's that supposed to mean?"

"I'll bet you can figure it out."

"I'm not going to play guessing games with you."

Mack shrugged and took another sip of his beer, aware that the background buzz of voices in the bar had ceased. The other patrons had stopped what they were doing to follow the conversation between Landon and the new guy.

He might have turned around to tell them to mind their own business, but he figured that wouldn't go over so well with this crowd, so he stayed with his back to the room.

"Get out of here," Landon said in a low voice.

"This is a free country."

"I don't like you and that daughter of Gloria's comin' around making trouble."

"What kind of trouble?"

"Whatever."

"Maybe you're the one making trouble."

"Oh yeah?"

Mack shrugged, hoping to get a rise out of the guy.

"I'm talking to you."

When Mack didn't answer, Landon pulled him around on the bar stool with his left hand and aimed a right hook at his chin.

Chapter Nine

Mack was ready for the move. He dodged the fist as he sprang up and leveled his own punch, catching Landon on the jaw. They were both standing now, both in the middle of a battle that Mack had provoked. Not because he wanted a violent confrontation but because he thought it was the only way to communicate with Landon.

He traded another round with the jerk, ducking to avoid a direct blow to his eye but catching a fist on the forehead. Landon didn't have much style, but he had the power to inflict damage.

As Mack was about to come back with another right, two men caught him from behind and held his arms. To the credit of the regulars in the bar, two of them also came up behind Landon and stopped him from delivering another punch.

The bartender looked from him to Landon and back again. "You come here to make trouble?" he asked.

"I came here for information."

"It sounds more like you came in to pick a fight."

Mack didn't answer.

"Unless you get the hell out of here, I'm going to call the cops. Is that what you want?"

"No," Mack muttered, sorry he hadn't thought his strategy through. He'd been keyed up for action and simply gone with gut instinct.

"Let me go," he said to the men in back of him.

"If you head for the door and don't do anything stupid on the way out," the bartender answered.

Mack jerked his head toward Landon. "What about him?"

"He comes here regular."

Mack sighed. It wasn't going to do him any good to argue the justice of the pronouncement.

Instead, he turned and walked toward the exit. He didn't rub his sore forehead until he'd gotten outside.

Someone behind him opened the door and looked out, probably to make sure he wasn't going to hang around and try to jump Landon later.

Mack walked across the street to his SUV, climbed in and drove away, thinking that he'd made a mess of that encounter. So much for his professional detective skills.

It was because of his own frustration, he thought. Frustration with himself, with Jamie, with the situation. He wanted to have a normal conversation with her, but she didn't want to talk to him. So he'd gone after Landon instead. What had he thought? That the guy was going to confess to trying to run her down? And when that hadn't worked, he'd returned and tried to shove her into his car? Then Mack would come back to Jamie with the news of the confession, and she'd leap into his arms in gratitude.

He snorted. If that had been the scenario, it hadn't panned out. Using the technique he'd employed with Jamie, he thought about the encounter. Landon's eyes were brown. But his nose wasn't anything remarkable.

Mack pulled into a gas station, bought a soft drink from the machine and held the icy can against his temple as he drove back to the hotel. With any luck, Jamie would be sleeping, and he wouldn't have to see her until the morning.

But when he tried to open the door, the interior latch stopped him, and he had to knock.

Through the crack in the door, he saw Jamie looking out, a wary expression on her face. When she saw it was him, she opened the door fully, and he stepped quickly inside, his head turned slightly away.

But she spotted the red mark on his forehead where Landon had hit him.

"What happened to you?"

"I walked into a door."

"I don't think so."

He sighed. "I tried to ask your mom's boyfriend some questions, and he didn't take kindly to my interfering with his evening."

"At Louie's Bar?"

"Yeah."

Her face had taken on a look that made his heart beat a little faster. "Worried about me?" he asked.

She took a moment before answering, "Yes."

He wasn't prepared for the catch in her voice. Instead of commenting on her reaction, he said, "I gave as good as I got."

She came back at him with a sharp retort. "That's just great. He's dangerous. And despite what we think of him, he's got friends in town. You should have stayed away from him."

Mack wasn't going to admit he'd done anything wrong. "I want to know if he's the guy who went after you."

"You said it was the killer."

"I said it could be the killer or Landon. There's still no way to be sure."

She made a small sound of distress. "I wish…"

"What?"

"I'd like to know if they were both the same guy." She straightened and gave him a closer inspection. "You need to put some ice on your forehead."

"Yeah." He walked toward the small refrigerator, bent and pulled out the ice tray, thinking the evening wasn't going the way he'd planned. Not at all. But had they made some sort of breakthrough in their personal communications? At least they were talking again. He should ask for clarification, except that he didn't know how to do it without maybe setting her off again. Damn, he hated feeling like he was trying to walk through a bed of hot coals without burning his toes.

After wrapping some cubes of ice in a dish towel, he turned back toward Jamie.

"Putting on the safety lock was a good idea," he said.

"Thanks."

"I thought you were sleeping."

"I decided to make some calls to people I know in town."

"And?"

"Some of them know Aubrey Rollins. I didn't get any bad reports on him. He's an aggressive real estate agent, but he hasn't made anyone mad. Actually, he's considered a good catch by the women my age."

"Okay."

She cleared her throat. "It felt like I wasn't getting anywhere with questions about him. Then I started thinking about something else." She paused a moment, then started again. "You remember we drove around looking for the funhouse, and I couldn't find it? Maybe there's another way."

"Like what?"

"Suppose I try to go there in my mind. The way I did in the dreams."

"You can do that?"

She hesitated. "I never tried it before."

"But you think you can do it now?"

"Yes."

"Why?"

"Because I've been there a couple of times already. I never did that in a dream before. I think it means I've got a connection to the place."

"I don't like it."

"Why not?"

"Because going there scares you. With good reason. It's not a nice place. I hate to have you do it deliberately."

"But I want to try." She cleared her throat. "And I waited until you came home. That was sensible, wasn't it?"

"Yes."

He studied her anxious expression. At first he'd thought that she couldn't possibly be getting any information about a murder with some kind of psychic mumbo jumbo. Then he'd come around to the point of view that there was no other way she could have known about it. Now the idea of her deliberately going to the site of two murders made his skin crawl, but if she'd done it once, maybe she could do it again. And so far they didn't have any other leads.

"You're sure you want to try it?"

She nodded.

"How do you want to do it?"

Some of the tension went out of her shoulders. "I guess the first thing I should do is get comfortable."

She sat down on the couch, leaned her head back against the cushion, and closed her eyes.

After watching her for a few moments, he asked, "Where should I be?"

Her eyes snapped open again, and he wondered if he'd broken her concentration.

"In one of the chairs," she answered in a barely audible voice.

He took the easy chair facing the sofa where he could easily monitor her.

JAMIE CLOSED HER eyes again and folded her hands in her lap. She took a deep breath and let it out. Then another. She could feel Mack across the room, watching her, and she wanted to ask him to go in the bedroom.

But she didn't do it, because she didn't want to be alone. But being alone, she reminded herself, was the only way she could do this. If she could do it at all.

She wasn't even sure what she was doing. Trying to sleep? Well, not a normal sleep. A sleep that would take her away from her body to another place.

As she sat on the sofa, she called up a picture of a hallway in the funhouse, trying to recapture the feeling she got when she was in one of the nightmares. Maybe that was too threatening, because nothing happened.

Switching tactics, she let her mind drift.

For a long time, she knew she was sitting on the couch, trying to do something that she didn't really understand.

Then she felt a change. It was like her mind was drifting away from her body.

A jolt of fear pulled her back, and she made a low sound.

"Jamie?"

That was Mack, calling to her. But his voice was far away, and she knew that only part of her was still in the hotel room.

She felt her lips form words. "I'm okay," she whispered, wondering if she'd spoken aloud so that he could hear her.

ALARM ZINGED THROUGH Mack as he watched Jamie. Her eyes were closed, but her face looked strange. Flat and smooth. Like she'd left her body sitting on the couch and gone somewhere else.

Well, wasn't that what she was trying to do?

She'd said she was all right.

Should he believe it?

The seconds ticked by, and nothing much seemed to change. Then she jerked a little and slumped to the side.

He started to jump up, then stopped himself. If she was really going to the funhouse, he'd pull her out of it.

He forced himself to stay where he was, watching her. Her body jerked again and slumped over more. He knew she was going to wake up with a kink in her neck if she stayed that way.

Quietly he stood and crossed to her.

"I'm going to pick you up," he murmured as he bent to slip one arm under her legs and the other in back of her shoulders.

Gathering her in his arms, he straightened and held her against his chest. She felt limp.

After making sure she was secure in his arms, he carried her to the bedroom.

The covers were already thrown back, and he laid her on the bottom sheet.

But he wasn't going to leave her there alone, because every other time she'd been to the place, she'd awakened in a panic. Quietly, he eased onto the bed beside her, then rolled onto his side so that he could watch her face.

She looked calm, until an expression of alarm crossed her features.

"What is it?" he whispered.

She opened her eyes and stared at him, although he wasn't sure she was really seeing him.

"Where am I?" she asked.

"You're with me. With Mack."

"No."

"Then where are you?"

"The funhouse. I think."

It was a strange conversation. Was she there or not?

Alarm sizzled through him. Could he wake her if he needed to? Maybe he should do it now.

He reached out a hand and pulled it back. If he woke her, he might be the cause of the experiment going wrong.

"Jamie," he whispered again.

Again she looked at him. Then her body began to shake.

"What's happening?"

"I'm cold."

"Wake up."

"No," she protested again. Then she was silent.

"Jamie. I don't like this. Jamie."

"IT'S ALL RIGHT," Jamie managed to say.

Was she talking to Mack? She was vaguely aware of him, of the hotel suite. She could feel the pillow and the sheet below her. She remembered that she'd been lying down and hadn't remade the bed. Then the room where her body was lying became less important as the funhouse became more real.

She shivered. It was cold in here. Nobody had turned on the heat.

She'd hoped to arrive outside so she could have some idea of where the house was. But she had come directly inside, into a wide front hall.

Whirling, she turned to look out the windows and found they were covered with opaque panels. When she clawed at them, they stayed in place.

Giving up the attempt to see outside, she walked farther into the house and found there were no open areas. As soon as she stepped out of the front hall, she was in a long corridor. Like the ones she remembered from the dreams.

She ran her hand along one wall, then the other. The left side was smooth plaster. The right was plywood.

Apparently he'd changed the structure of the house to create the environment he wanted, but not permanently.

She glanced back over her shoulder. She could walk down the hallway…but what if she got trapped? What if he came up behind her?

Could he catch her here the way he had caught his other victims? But she wasn't really here, was she? Surely she'd be able to leave the same way she'd come.

She wished she had a flashlight. To her amazement, her fist closed around something cold and cylindrical.

The object she'd wished for.

That emboldened her. This wasn't reality, nor was it exactly one of her dreams. There must be different rules because she'd brought herself here. She had control of the situation. Or at least that was the best explanation she could come up with.

She clicked on the light and shined it on the walls, examining them more closely. She could see the nails in the plywood. And on the plaster side, she could see a high, old-fashioned baseboard.

She kept walking, shining the light ahead of her. There were little doors in the walls, like doors to cabinets, and when she opened one, a monster with green skin, red glowing eyes and black horns sprang out at her.

With a muffled cry, she jumped back. Even as she did, she knew the monster wasn't real. But she was too on edge for that to matter.

When she reached for it, the texture was sticky, like

a nest of spiderwebs, and she dropped the thing with a grimace, watching the head bounce back and forth. She should put it back before the guy who owned this place noticed.

She laughed, the sound echoing through the hallway. How could he notice? This was her dream. She wasn't really here. Or was she?

She couldn't be sure of that or sure of anything—except that this place gave her the creeps, and she wanted to get away.

But she'd discovered a way of coming here, and it would be stupid to leave without finding out anything useful. Maybe if she got to the back of the house, she'd find some windows. Or maybe the upstairs hadn't been turned into a funhouse. Maybe it was normal and she could see outside from there.

She looked back toward the entry hall where she'd seen a staircase. Should she go up?

The idea sent a shiver over her skin. Maybe he was up there. Maybe that's where he went when no one else was here. He wouldn't need a mask. She'd be able to see his face. But the idea of confronting him made her heart pound.

Instead, she kept walking down the corridor.

When she came to a place where the hallway hit a wall and a perpendicular passage, she stopped, remembering one of her previous dreams. The other women who had been here had faced a choice like that—left or right—and it hadn't worked out so well for them.

Stopping, Jamie shone the beam down the hallway to the left, seeing it stretch away before her. It looked like the corridor went on for at least twenty feet before it made a turn. Next she lowered the beam and made a small sound when the light picked up a thin line on the floor on the right-hand side. Getting down on her hands and knees, she reached out and pressed against the floor. It wasn't solid. At her touch, it pushed downward, allowing a musty smell to drift upward toward her. Shining the light into the hole, she saw a yawning black cavern below her. But the choking dampness made her cough, and she quickly eased the trapdoor back into place.

It made a sucking noise, and she went still, hoping he hadn't heard it. Only, how could he? This was simply her dream of the funhouse, although that didn't make the place less dangerous. If she'd been walking down the corridor without being on her guard, she would have fallen through to the floor below. Would she have gotten hurt? She couldn't answer that question.

Fighting the feeling of being trapped, she slid down the wall and landed in a little heap on the floor where she pulled up her knees and rested her chin on them.

This excursion had been her idea, and now she desperately wanted to escape from this place. Too bad she didn't know how to get back to the real world.

She sat there for long moments, struggling to wake herself up. But apparently it wasn't going to work.

What if she called out to Mack? Would he hear her?

She tried it, but she didn't seem to get any response. She must be too far into the dream to reach him.

Finally, with a sigh, she climbed to her feet again, then turned and retraced her steps, looking for the way out just as the other women had searched for an exit. Only they hadn't found it.

When she came to a door, she opened it. Shining the light beyond, she saw a large room. In the center was an ornately carved wooden table perhaps four feet wide and eight feet long. Around it were chairs in some kind of antique style that she couldn't name.

Was this the old dining room to the house? A place that had nothing to do with frightening people.

Cautiously, she stepped through the opening. The door slammed closed behind her, and suddenly the chamber was full of flashing lights and blaring sound. Black light shone on the table and chairs, turning them an eerie green. And music that sounded like the soundtrack of a horror movie blasted out at her.

From above her, a giant spider descended, its eyes glowing red. When it reached the table, it started bouncing around.

She gagged and jumped back, then turned to press on the door. This time it wouldn't open.

What had made her think she could come here with no consequences? She was trapped. Just like the other women had been trapped.

No, she told herself. All she had to do was wake up. But that was beyond her power.

Desperately, she looked around the room and spotted another doorway at the far side. She was making her way around the table, when one of the chairs pulled out by itself, as though a ghost had gotten up from the table. Unprepared for the movement, she bashed into the chair, whacking her shin.

But she wasn't going to let it stop her from escaping. She couldn't give up, because that would be death.

She wanted to cover her ears and close her eyes, to blot out the flashing lights and the terrible music. Only that would leave her blind and deaf.

Gritting her teeth, she grabbed the back of another chair. Maybe if she sat down, she'd feel better. But when she pulled it away from the table, she gasped. The seat was covered with knife blades, sticking upward. If she'd sat down, they would have cut her terribly. She jumped back, hitting the wall, and it seemed to come alive with ghostly hands pulling at her arms and shoulders.

MACK'S FEAR ROSE AS he watched Jamie writhe on the bed, her arms flailing.

He rolled toward her, holding her arms at her sides so she wouldn't bash him in the face. "Sweetheart, wake up."

In response, her panic seemed to surge, along with his own. She had wanted to do this. Now he was afraid that it could kill her.

Fear made his stomach knot.

A dream could kill her? He wouldn't have thought it possible. Until now.

"Let me go," she moaned, and he was sure she didn't know he was holding her.

What should he do? He rolled away from her and eased off the bed, where she wasn't going to hit him. Her head rolled from side to side, and he wondered if she knew where she was.

He didn't know if she was here with him or trapped in a dream world. He'd never experienced anything like this, and he simply didn't know what to do.

When she screamed, he came back to the bed and tried to gather her close, but she kept screaming, kept trying to jerk herself out of his arms, her back arching in her struggle to get away.

Terrified, he tried to get through to her.

"Jamie. Sweetheart. Come back to me."

She didn't seem to hear. Didn't seem to know he was even there.

"Jamie!"

She kept struggling, and when he pressed his hand to her chest, he could feel her heart beating wildly.

What should he do?

SCREAMING, SHE TRIED TO pull away, but the living wall held her in its grip.

She shouldn't be here. Coming to this place had been a terrible mistake. If she could have clawed her way out, she would have fled the dream. But it continued to hold her fast.

And then something worse happened. To her right, she heard a noise. Jerking away from the wall, she turned to face the door. Not the one where she'd entered. Another door.

It opened to reveal the figure of a man.

She had seen him before. At least twice.

He was dressed all in black, with a cape flowing out behind him as though a strong breeze were blowing it. In place of a face, he had a death mask.

"You," he whispered. "How did you get here?"

Her only answer was a scream.

She would have run, but her feet were rooted to the floor.

The figure came toward her. Far away, she heard someone calling her name. It was Mack.

"Jamie. Wake up, Jamie."

"I can't," she whispered.

Mack spoke again, his voice urgent. "Yes, you can. Jamie, come back to me."

She wanted to. She wanted to get out of this awful place. She wanted to come back to him.

"Keep talking to me," she whispered because she knew that he was her link to sanity, and only he could drag her back to the real world.

"Jamie. Sweetheart. Please, Jamie."

She felt Mack's hand clamp around hers. Sensed his desperation.

Somehow she managed to turn her hand, knitting her fingers with his, clinging to his solid flesh and bone. He was real. The only thing that was real. The rest of it was only a nightmare.

"Yes! Wake up."

She could hear him. Touch him. But she couldn't see him. All she could see was the man in black with the death mask coming around the table, advancing on her step by step like the murderer in a horror movie. He was going to swoop down on her, and that would be the end.

She felt herself lifted, and she knew deep in her mind that it wasn't the monster who had her. It was Mack. He was carrying her somewhere.

He shifted her weight, seemed to lower her, triggering a roaring noise in her ears. A confusion of impressions assaulted her. But one thing she knew above all others, the bad man was still in back of her. Coming. He was going to grab her the way he had grabbed the other women. And there was no escape. He would kill her, just the way he'd killed the rest of his victims.

Chapter Ten

The monster was almost there, reaching out his hands toward her. He was going to seize her.

Then something wet came pouring down on her, soaking her to the skin.

She started coughing, and sputtering. When she opened her eyes, she blinked in confusion. She was in the shower. With her clothes on. Mack was holding her in his arms. He was in the shower, too, standing there fully dressed with water pouring down on them.

"Thank God," he muttered.

"What...what happened?" she choked out.

"You were screaming. I think he was coming at you, but you couldn't wake up. I tried to make you hear me, but I couldn't do it."

"I did hear you. I knew you were there," she whispered. "I could feel your hands on me, but I couldn't get to you."

"I thought if I got you wet, that would be enough of a shock to make you come back to the world."

Water was still pouring out of the showerhead onto them.

She laughed. "I guess it worked."

"Yeah." He set her on her feet, made sure she was steady, then reached to turn off the water. "Sorry."

"About what?"

"Dousing you."

"It was the right thing to do."

He pulled her close, wrapping his arms around her, swaying with her in the tub, saying her name over and over.

She heard him swallow. "I was scared. Scared you were stuck there."

"I think I might have been, if you hadn't pulled me out."

He nodded against the top of her head.

"What happened, exactly?"

"I went to the funhouse. Like in my dreams. Only it was different."

"Did you find out where the place was?"

"No. I was inside the whole time." She gulped. "I was like the women he'd brought there. Only I had…abilities they didn't."

"What do you mean?"

"I wished I had a flashlight, and then I was holding one. The way it can happen in a dream."

He nodded.

"First I was inside the main entrance to the house." She thought for a moment. "I think he'd left it the way he found it, but he'd made a longer hallway beyond that. I went down it. There was a trapdoor in the floor. But I found it and kept going. Then I stepped into a…dining room."

"Like a regular dining room?"

She shook her head. "There was a table and chairs, but it was set up like a spook show, and the door locked behind me. When it wouldn't open again, I walked around the table." She gulped. "Then all of the sudden he was there—coming through another doorway. He was coming toward me. You got me out of there just in time."

Mack ran his fingers up and down her arm reassuringly. "It wasn't real."

"You can say that." She shuddered. "I don't know if it's true. I mean, the rules aren't like the real world—or like regular dreams."

"Did you see his face?"

"He had on a mask."

"The ski mask? Like when he pushed you into the car?"

"No. The death mask like when he went after the other women." She made a strangled sound. "He looked like he did when he was with the women, telling them they could get away. Only we both know they couldn't escape."

"He wasn't really there. How could he be, in your dream?"

She sucked in a breath. "He recognized me."

His hands clenched on her shoulders. "How do you know?"

"He said…'you'."

"But not your name?"

"No."

"Then he could have meant someone else."

She knew there was no point in arguing with Mack about what was real and what was not. He hadn't been there. He didn't understand that what had happened to her in the funhouse had taken on a life of its own.

"I was so scared," she murmured.

"So was I."

She nodded. She's known it even when she was dreaming. She knew it now.

Mack's voice turned gentle. "We'd better get dry," he said, leaning her shoulders against the tile wall and taking a step back. He was fumbling with the buttons on the front of her shirt, when his hands went still.

"Maybe I shouldn't be undressing you," he said in a thick voice.

When he met her gaze, she didn't look away. "Maybe you should," she said, her own voice equally thick.

"Why?"

"You saved me."

His voice turned rough. "You don't have to pay me back."

"That's not what I meant." She swallowed hard. "I mean you were my lifeline—the reason I wanted to come back. You were the thing in this world I could cling to. Even when I was in that place, in some ways I knew I was here with you. I don't know what would have happened if I'd tried to do it before you came back. I guess I realized it was too dangerous without you."

She reached for him, the wet fabric of their clothing slapping together. After a long moment, she eased away and began working at her shirt buttons.

When she raised her head, the look in his eyes made her chest go tight with need.

"After what happened, you need to rest."

She knew that he was saying it because he thought it was the right thing to do.

"I think I know what I need," she answered. "You."

She cupped her hand around the back of his head and brought his mouth down to hers, and when their lips touched, she knew that was the right move.

Her wet clothing had turned cold, chilling her to the bone. But when he moved his lips against hers, heat sizzled through her body.

She opened her mouth to give him better access, silently saying that she needed him.

"I was so scared when I couldn't wake you," he whispered against her mouth.

"I know. I'm sorry."

"I had to do something. And the only thing I thought of was to carry you to the shower."

"That was smart."

"And now I'm taking advantage of you."

"No."

"You're sure?"

"Very."

In answer his hand slid down to her hips, pressing her against the hard shaft of his erection.

"We've got to get out of these wet clothes," he muttered.

Because she'd been in bed, she was wearing sweatpants. All he had to do was slip his hands inside the elastic and pull them down, along with her panties.

When they pooled around her feet, she stepped out of them, and he ran his hands over the curve of her bottom, then lower, to find her sex. She was already aroused, and he made a low sound in his throat as he stroked her there.

"I don't think I can stand up much longer," she whispered.

"I know the feeling. Give me a second."

He pulled his dripping shirt over his head while she got rid of her bra, then reached for the snap at the top of his jeans.

When she had trouble lowering the zipper, he helped her, his erection bouncing out as he freed it.

Naked, they clung together, swaying in the tub.

"Bedroom," she whispered.

They left a sodden mass of clothing in the tub as they staggered back to the bedroom, where they fell onto the bed together. He gathered her close, stroking his fingers over her back, down her flanks, pulling her against his body, making her feel like every tender part of her was going to ignite.

Easing away, he took her breasts in his hands, his thumbs stroking over the hardened tips, bringing a whimper to her lips.

He sucked one taut nipple into his mouth, while he slid his hand down her body into the folds of her sex, his fingers knowing and skillful. His hands and mouth sent pleasure roaring through her body.

"Now," she whispered, closing her fist around him, making it impossible to deny what they both wanted.

When she rolled to her back, he followed, letting her guide him inside her.

They both exclaimed at the joining. Then he began to move, making her cry out again as she came undone for him.

He followed her over the edge, and she clasped her arms around his shoulders, hugging him to her. She had reached for him, and he had taken her in his arms and given her what she needed. She wanted him to know that it had been the right thing to do.

"Thank you," she whispered.

"Thank you," he answered, and she heard the emotion in his voice. It made her chest tighten. This meant a lot to him. More than she ever would have believed.

And what about her, she thought. Tomorrow would she regret what they had done?

FRED HYDE STOOD IN the dining room of his magnificent creation. He'd been sleeping upstairs when something had wakened him. It wasn't his alarm going off. It was something else, something he couldn't explain beyond a sudden sense of dread.

He'd jumped out of bed and inspected the system. It was functioning properly and showed no intrusions.

No one had gotten into the house. He was sure of that. Yet he was still feeling nervous, as though a presence that didn't belong was here. After dressing quickly, he went down to walk around the first floor. Everything seemed to be in order, yet when he entered the dining room, a shivery feeling rippled over his skin. It was like that feeling they call "someone walking over your grave." Ridiculous.

He had the house rigged so that you couldn't turn on the lights in the normal way at the switches. You had to use his remote control, which he did before making sure nothing was out of place.

When he got to the dining room table, he stopped and stared. There was a mechanism in the floor that triggered a latch in the ceiling. When you stepped in the right place, a spider came down a thread of web and landed in the middle of the table where it jumped around like it was going to spring off the table and take a chomp out of your arm. Only it never left the horizontal surface.

There was no reason it should have fallen to the table now. Only here it was. And he'd have to put it back. Or get out one of the birds with the steel claws and knife-blade beaks.

There was something else that stopped him in his tracks. One of the chairs was standing away from the table. And he was sure he had pushed them all in.

What the hell was going on?

He stood very still, thinking. Trying to pick up vibrations, if one could do something like that. He didn't believe in paranormal stuff, even though he'd made the funhouse into a place where otherworldly phenomena seemed to be part of the landscape. But it was all fake. All from his own imagination or stuff he'd seen in movies or read in books.

Once again he assured himself that nobody could have been here, yet it felt like someone had been in the house. Here in this room, messing with his creation.

Closing his eyes, he tried to conjure up an image of who it might have been... and lit on Jamie Shepherd.

Impossible. She didn't even know where this place was. Still, another shiver went up his spine. He'd have to capture her before she wrecked all his plans.

Could she?

What if she and that detective started sharing information with the cops?

But what did they know, really? What could they know?

MACK WOKE AND CAUTIOUSLY turned his head. Jamie was lying next to him, staring at the ceiling.

"You okay?" he asked, hearing the catch in his voice.

"I'm not going to jump out of bed and run away from you," she said.

"That's something," he managed to answer as he allowed himself to relax a little.

Under the covers, she found his hand and knit his fingers with hers. "But I do want you to understand something."

He was immediately on edge again.

"About what happened to me last night. When I went to the funhouse."

"Okay."

"It was real, in a way that I can't explain to you."

"Okay," he said again, wondering why she was insisting. Then it hit him. This could be a test. Maybe not a conscious one on her part, but a test nonetheless. They'd made love, and it had been wonderful, but there had to be more to their relationship than great sex. There had to be trust. He'd been a little in love with her since Craig first brought her back to Baltimore from Gaptown. Back then he'd seen her as a charming, desirable, funny, smart woman. He hadn't known there was another dimension to her. Something that she'd kept hidden because she realized that it was hard for people to accept.

He knew she must have told Craig about her strange ability. Before or after he'd brought her to Baltimore, he wondered. At any rate, he was sure Craig had accepted it.

And he would have to do the same, if he wanted his relationship with Jamie to go anywhere.

"What are you thinking?"

He swallowed. "That I'd like to understand what the dream meant to you."

Her face was so serious that he felt his stomach clench. "It was weird."

"I'll bet." He tightened his hold on her hand. "Tell me what you can about it."

"Before, when I dreamed about something bad happening to another person, I was always that person, experiencing it through their senses. This time, it was just me, alone in the dream, and that somehow made it worse." She tensed. "Well, I was alone until he came in at the end."

She was silent for a moment, and he didn't press her, just let her tell it the way she wanted to.

"The worst part was that I had the absolute feeling that I was really there. I mean, if I go to the house, it will be exactly like the dream. Unless he changes something around in the meantime."

She sank back against the pillows, took a deep breath and let it out. "I said the worst part was feeling like it was so real, but maybe that's not true. Maybe the worst part is that I put myself through hell, and I don't have any better idea where to find the house than when I started."

"It's okay."

"It's not. I failed."

"No. You thought it would work. It was a reasonable thing to try."

"I thought maybe I'd get there and be outside. But I was in the entrance hall."

"You still think the house is out in the country?"

She hesitated. "I don't know."

"What's different?"

"I just have the feeling that I wasn't all that far from here. And…" She huffed out a breath. "There's the way he set up the area inside at the front door. If the house were in the country, maybe nobody would come around. But I think he decided he had to have the entry looking normal. I mean, if someone rang the bell, and he opened the door, they'd see a vestibule that looked like part of an ordinary house. So he was thinking that maybe somebody would come to the door. I know that's kind of going in circles, but do you know what I mean?"

"I think so."

She made a frustrated sound. "My clever idea of dreaming a visit there didn't work. Let's go back to plan A."

Jamie waited for Mack to challenge her.

All he said was, "What's plan A?"

She breathed out a little sigh. "Figuring out a link between the victims."

"Okay. But first we need something to eat."

"Yeah."

She started to throw back the covers and realized she was naked.

"I'll get you something," Mack said.

He climbed out of bed, went to the closet, and brought her the dress shirt he'd hung there, in case he needed it.

Before she could say anything, he grabbed a pair of jeans and walked into the sitting room, giving her an excellent view of his muscled body.

Jamie sat up and pulled on the shirt, feeling a little strange about wearing his clothing.

Was he putting his brand on her, or had he just picked something that would cover her up?

She pulled a pair of panties from her suitcase and put them on, then walked into the front room.

This was no normal morning after. She'd had the clever idea of dreaming herself into the funhouse. It hadn't worked out the way she'd thought. Neither had the next part. She'd ended up making love with Mack, and she wasn't going to tell herself it hadn't been good. Too good, actually.

She needed a little space, but they were stuck together in this hotel suite, and she couldn't go outside to get away from him because that tactic hadn't worked out so well, either.

Maybe breakfast would distract her. Breakfast was normal, right?

He'd already pulled on a T-shirt and put two bowls and the box of cereal they'd bought on the table. She got milk from the small refrigerator, while he made coffee using the packets the hotel had provided.

"Orange juice?" he asked.

"A little," she answered.

Still uncomfortable, she crossed to the coffee table and picked up the notes she'd made on the murder victims along with some newspaper pages she'd printed from the library files. Most of them were about the funhouse case, but she also had the article that involved Craig.

Back at the dinette table, she shuffled through the papers as she drank her coffee, then suddenly set the cup down with a thunk.

"What?" Mack asked.

She could feel the tightness in her chest when she looked up. "I told you I met Craig when he came to Gaptown on a case."

"Uh-huh," he answered, and she could see he was suddenly on the alert. He was probably wondering why she had to bring up Craig now.

"He came here investigating insurance frauds. Then he came back for something else. A kidnapping." She turned her palm up. "When we were at the library, I…uh…saw an article about the second case and printed it."

"Why?"

"I…just did." She raised her shoulder. "It made me feel closer to him."

He wrapped his hands around his coffee cup. "Okay."

"Did you know about either case he was working on here?"

Mack shook his head.

"When he came back to town, he was chasing a man who was estranged from his wife and had snatched their son. The guy was driving west in a bad rainstorm. Maybe he was going to stop here for the night or something. But when he got off the highway in Gaptown, he was in a one-car accident."

Mack nodded.

"He skidded and hit a light pole. His car was wrecked. His son was injured and taken to the emergency room."

"Do I need to know all those details?" he asked, his voice tight.

"I'm giving you the background. They quote the emergency room nurse in the article. The nurse was Lynn Vaughn."

He almost sloshed coffee into his cereal bowl.

"Lynn Vaughn?" he repeated.

"Yes."

"What did she say?"

Jamie passed the paper to him, and he quickly scanned the article.

Lynn hadn't said much, only that the boy, Billy Fried, had been brought in and then released. Because his father was in police custody, the child had been turned over to county social services.

She watched Mack read through the article. "There's nothing else of interest," he said.

"Don't you think it's weird that it mentions Lynn Vaughn?" she pressed.

He shrugged. "I guess she was on shift that night."

"Maybe. But I think we should look through later papers to find out what happened," she said.

"Why should we? Don't you think it's just a coincidence?" he snapped.

"It could be, but I can't shake the feeling that it may be more."

He looked like he was fighting the impulse to snap at her again, and she was sorry she'd put him on edge.

When he spoke, he answered in an even tone. "I guess we can go back to the library."

"But you don't think we should bother?"

"You're suggesting it could be a lead in this case."

"I think it could be." She shrugged. "Let's call it a strong hunch."

They'd run out of things to say to each other and ate the remainder of the meal in silence. When they were finished Jamie got up to put the dishes in the sink.

"You get dressed. I'll wash them," Mack said.

"Thanks," she answered, wondering if he was trying to be nice or trying to show her how helpful he could be.

At the entrance to the bedroom, she turned to see him getting the bottle of dishwashing liquid out of the bottom cabinet.

Before he turned around and caught her watching him, she closed the door and got a clean shirt and a pair of jeans from her suitcase.

Beside her was the bed where they'd slept together. It still didn't feel right to have had such a wonderful time in his arms, but it didn't feel all that wrong, either.

What was so bad about going on with her life, she asked herself. Wouldn't Craig want her to do that?

Or was it bad because she'd known that Mack was attracted to his friend's wife? She'd been kind of attracted to him, too. Certainly she'd noticed him among the Light Street detectives and Randolph Security men she'd met at parties. But she'd made sure it stayed on a superficial level with Mack Steele because she was married to Craig. Now, everything had changed, but she was having trouble coping with the new reality.

She took a quick shower, pulled on her underwear, then hung the wet clothes in the bathroom over the towel racks. Cautiously, she opened the door and stuck her head out. Mack must have decided to stay out of the bedroom until she was done because he was nowhere in sight.

She grabbed her clothes, finished dressing in the bathroom, then cleared out. When she came back to the living room, Mack was staring out the window. From the way his shoulders tensed, she knew he'd heard her.

"What are you doing?"

He turned to face her. "Scanning the parking lot for suspicious-looking cars."

"You see anything we should worry about?"

"No. But I'm still thinking about whether to change hotels again."

"It gets kind of wearing, moving every night. Why don't we just stay here? There aren't a lot of choices in town. Anybody that could find me at this place could find me somewhere else. Or do you want to go to the Bruce House? It's a B and B."

"Under the circumstances, we're probably better off not having to make breakfast conversation with other guests."

"Good point."

When he went to get dressed, she took his spot at the window, looking out until he came back about fifteen minutes later.

"See anything we should worry about?" he asked when he returned.

"Nothing obvious. But I'm probably not as good as you are at spotting trouble."

"I was thinking we'd go to the library to check the local papers again," Mack said. "But while I was taking a shower, I came up with something else we could try."

"Which is?"

"We never looked up Jeanette Baker's specialty."

He sat down on the couch, opened his laptop and turned on the machine.

While he waited for the computer to boot up, Jamie paced back and forth across the living room. Mack glanced at her but didn't complain.

Then he began typing, and she sat down beside him, waiting while he went to Google.

When he found Jeanette Baker's obituary, he scanned the entry.

Jamie made a small sound when she saw that Jeanette

had worked for Allegany County social services in the Children's Division.

"Oh Lord. I guess you're thinking the same thing I am."

"That she was the one who took custody of Billy Fried."

"Can you find that out?"

"Maybe."

He got out of the website and went into another, this one linked directly to the child services division of the county system. Jamie sat tensely next to him until a screen popped up with the answer. Jeanette Baker had been the social worker assigned to the little boy.

"That's the link between them," Jamie breathed. "They were both involved in the kidnapping case that brought Craig back here."

"Yeah."

She gasped as another terrible thought struck her. "He was killed by a hit and run driver. Do you think that could be connected?"

"It could be," he said, the words coming out low and grating.

"Oh Lord," she said again. "Oh Lord."

Mack reached for her hand, but she sprang off the sofa. "I'm sorry. I…"

She charged into the bedroom and closed the door, looking at the bed for a long moment. The bed where she and Mack had made love. She'd almost convinced herself that it was okay. Now she knew that she and Mack were involved in the case that Craig had been investigating.

Was that why he'd been killed? And by the same guy who had gone after Jeanette and Lynn Vaughn? It seemed impossible that those three people were linked up. But at the same time, it had come to make a kind of horrible sense.

With a trembling hand, she reached to straighten the covers. When the bed was more or less back together, she crawled in, still with her clothes on.

As a little girl, getting under the covers and feeling their weight on top of her had always been comforting. The habit had persisted into adulthood.

Numbly, she pulled the sheet, blanket and spread up to her chin, making a cocoon for herself as she felt hot tears well in her eyes. She didn't try to stop them, but she sure as hell hoped that Mack wasn't coming in here.

She let the misery flow out because she was helpless to do anything else. All the pain of Craig's death flowed over her again.

A long time later, a knock at the door woke her, and she realized she'd fallen asleep.

She pushed herself up and ran an unsteady hand through her hair. When she looked at the clock, she saw that three hours had passed. Somehow she'd slept that long. Probably because she couldn't face reality.

"Are you all right?" Mack called out.

"Yes," she forced herself to say.

He waited a long moment before asking, "Can you come out? I've found out something else about the case."

"What?"

"It's a little inconvenient talking through a closed door."

"Okay. Just a minute." She heaved herself out of bed, then staggered into the bathroom where she used the facilities, splashed water on her face and ran a comb through her hair. She still looked like hell, but she didn't particularly care.

Feeling uncertain about facing Mack, she walked stiffly

to the door and opened it. He was sitting where she'd left him on the couch. The computer was still on his lap.

He looked up, and she felt his gaze.

Ignoring the scrutiny, she crossed the room, sat down in one of the dinette chairs and folded her arms across her middle.

When she didn't speak, he asked, "I did a bunch of research on the case. Are you going to get upset if we discuss it?"

She struggled to keep her voice even. "I hope not."

"Is there anything I can do for you?"

"No. Just tell me what you found."

She saw him swallow and knew that he wanted to talk about the two of them, but she wasn't going to let him do it. Not now.

"I think I've figured out the link between the three victims."

"You mean four, don't you? Because I believe we both know that Craig was killed by the same person."

Chapter Eleven

Mack kept his voice even. "All right, four." He pointed to some notes he'd made. "The father of the boy was named Henry Fried. He was tried in court here in Gaptown on the kidnapping charge. He got six years because it was a domestic case, but he got out early on parole." He paused and gave her a direct look. "The foreman of the jury that convicted him was Tim Conrad."

She felt a wave of cold sweep over her. "They're all linked to that case."

"Yeah."

"So we have to assume the person who killed the three people here and Craig in Baltimore is Henry Fried."

"Yes."

Her voice hardened as she felt a new sense of purpose take hold. "We can find him!"

"Unfortunately, not right away."

"Why not?"

"He seems to have dropped off the face of the earth."

"He's not dead! He's killing people."

"He must be using a different name."

She dragged in a breath and let it out, consciously making her voice less strident as she fought to control her emotions. Getting upset wasn't going to do her any good.

She needed to stay calm and focus on facts. "I guess that makes sense. What do we know about him?"

"He was an engineer with a good paying job—working for a high-tech waste management firm in Baltimore. Until his marriage went sour."

"An engineer. So he's technically oriented. He could have designed the…exhibits in his funhouse."

Mack nodded.

"But we still haven't found the house." She got up and paced to the window, then back toward the hallway, sorry that she'd bailed out and left Mack to do all the work. She'd come to Gaptown because she wanted to be part of the process. This morning, she'd freaked out over the knowledge that the same guy had murdered her husband. But that only gave her a more urgent reason to figure out who had killed Lynn Vaughn, Jeanette Baker and Tim Conrad. They'd also find Craig's killer. A while ago, she'd been too upset to realize that. Now she was determined to get the guy.

"What else did you get on him?" she asked, sitting down next to Mack.

"His wife's name. It's Helen Fried."

"Did you talk to her?"

"I wish I could have. But after she got her son back, she kept getting threatening communications from Fried."

"While he was in jail?"

"Yes. Eventually, she and the boy disappeared. I can't get a line on her. Which makes me think that's what her ex-husband's mad about. She took the boy somewhere he can never find him, and he's angry with all the people involved in the case here in Gaptown. Didn't you say he told the women they'd ruined his life?"

"Yes, but it's his fault, not theirs."

"According to standard logic. According to his logic, they stole his son away from him."

She pondered that. "He's getting revenge against them."

"It looks like it. I've been searching the web since you…" He stopped and started again. "I haven't come up with any leads on him. He's gone underground, and I'm not sure how to figure out who he is."

"The funhouse is around here. We could check real estate records."

"We'd have to check a lot of records. And we don't even know if he bought the house, rented it, or found an abandoned place and moved in. Still, real estate transactions might be our best option."

She nodded.

Mack sighed. "I need to knock off for a while. I'll go out and get some food and bring it back."

She gave him a considering look. He'd been at this for hours, and she'd been sleeping. "Okay," she said softly.

"You need to eat, too."

"I'm not hungry."

"Not eating isn't doing Craig any good," he said, his gaze drilling into her.

Her voice turned fierce. "What's that supposed to mean?"

"It means that your husband is dead, and you should keep your strength up if you want to find the guy who killed him."

She glared at him, wanting to ask what her eating had to do with it, but she did understand the logic of keeping herself in good shape.

"What are you going to get?" she asked.

"What do you want?"

She turned one hand palm up. "I don't care."

"I saw a Mexican-style fast food restaurant when we were driving around downtown. I can bring us back tacos or burritos. Which do you want?"

"Either is fine with me."

His eyes narrowed. "Stop acting like nothing matters to you any more."

"Stop telling me what to do," she shouted, then wished she hadn't raised her voice.

They stood staring at each other for charged moments. Finally, he turned and walked toward the door. In the hallway, he paused. "I'll be back as soon as I can. Keep the security lock on the door."

"Of course."

When he'd left, she pushed the safety bar into place, then stood for a few minutes with her back against the door.

She knew Mack was trying the best he could to solve the murders and also to give her the space she needed.

She went back to the bedroom, fixed the bed, then restlessly walked around the suite.

MACK DROVE AROUND the downtown area, looking for the taco joint he'd seen before. He was beginning to think he'd dreamed it up.

Finally he saw the sign in the distance. Only it was on a one-way street, and he had to circle back, cursing that nothing was going right at the moment.

Well, he couldn't say nothing. They had made some progress on the case, thanks to Jamie's printing that article about Craig, then insisting that he check up on Jeanette Baker. Was that a psychic insight?

He sighed. Maybe if he'd been alone, he would have had the same spooky feeling when he'd seen Lynn Vaughn's name in that article and started digging on his own. Only he wouldn't have looked at that article in the first place.

Too bad they had no idea what name Fried was using now. That was going to make finding him a little difficult. Perhaps it was time to go to the police with the information they had, but he couldn't do that without consulting Jamie.

Of course, he and Jamie had a lot more to talk about than just the case, if either one of them was up to it. He'd thought he had started building a relationship with her. Then Craig Shepherd had jumped back into the picture and changed everything.

He sighed. He and Craig had been good friends—which didn't make any of this easier. They'd all thought Craig had died in an accident. Now it looked like he'd been murdered. Catching the killer would mean a lot to Mack—for his own satisfaction and for Jamie. He knew this was tearing her up. That was perfectly obvious.

But had everything changed between himself and Jamie now? Were they back to the way things had been before this trip?

"Damn."

He slapped his hands against the steering wheel, then ordered himself to calm down. He'd waited a long time to reach out toward Jamie. He'd gotten through to her. He could do it again.

Unless she had decided to totally shut him out because she couldn't cope with anything besides her husband's murder.

WHEN JAMIE'S CELL PHONE rang, she jumped, then dug it out of her purse. It was probably Mack calling about dinner.

When she looked at the phone number, she sucked in a sharp breath. It wasn't Mack calling.

She considered not answering. Then she changed her mind and pushed the button.

"Mom?"

"Jamie! Thank God."

Her mother sounded frantic and breathless.

Alarm leaped in Jamie's chest. "Mom, what is it?"

"You've got to come over here right away."

'What's wrong? Did Clark do something to you?"

"I can't talk about it over the phone. You've got to come here. Right now."

She thought about what to do. "I'm at a hotel downtown. Mack is out getting us dinner. I don't have a car."

"Can't you take a cab?"

"You need me right away?"

"Yes. Please, Jamie. It's…urgent."

"Okay. I'll be there as soon as I can."

Jamie looked around the room, found the hotel notepad and scrawled a message for Mack: "My mom's in some kind of trouble. I'm going over there."

Then she called the front desk.

"This is Jamie Shepherd in room 524. Can you call me a cab?"

"Certainly."

"How long will it take?"

"Maybe five minutes."

She got out her cell phone again, but she'd never put Mack's number into her memory, and since she hadn't gotten any calls from him on the phone, she couldn't get his number that way either. The note would have to do.

As she rode down in the elevator, she went back over the call from her mother. Gloria had sounded frantic, but there was no way to know what was wrong. Not until she got there.

She wished Mack were with her, and with that thought came the realization that she was starting to depend on him. Or to put it another way, she knew she could depend on him.

Probably he was going to be angry that she'd gone out. Well, she'd deal with that after she found out what was wrong at home.

When she got to the lobby, she started for the front door, then stopped. She hated to be looking over her shoulder every second, but she knew Fried could be lurking out there.

Instead, she waited inside, until she saw a cab pull up at the door. Then she hurried across the lobby and exited the building.

Before she got in the cab, she gave the driver a long look, but he was a short, pudgy guy. Nothing like the man she'd seen in her dream trips to the funhouse.

"Where to?"

She told him her mother's address and sat back, trying to calm the pounding of her heart. She'd been telling herself for years that she didn't care what happened to Gloria Wheeler. Apparently she had been fooling herself.

It was only a short ride to her mom's place. When the cab arrived, she stared at the property. Clark's truck wasn't in the driveway, but he could have moved the vehicle somewhere else. After paying the driver, she got out and started up the sidewalk. The curtains in the front window were drawn, and the front door was closed.

Jamie tried the knob and found the door was unlocked. Cautiously, she pushed it open and peered into the cluttered living room.

The lights were on, but the room was empty.

"Mom?"

As she stepped inside, she heard a muffled noise from the bedroom.

"Mom?"

She hurried across the room and down the short hall, then stopped abruptly.

Her mother was sitting in one of the dinette chairs, her hands tied behind her back and a gag in her mouth. When she saw Jamie, her eyes went wide.

Jamie had started toward her when she heard a harsh voice from behind her. "Stop right there. Put your hands in the air if you don't want to get shot right now."

MACK KNOCKED ON THE hotel room door. When nobody answered, he knocked louder and called out, "Jamie?"

When she didn't answer, his heart started to pound.

Setting the bags with the tacos down on the carpet beside the door, he fished his key card out of his pocket, unlocked the door and charged into the living room. It was empty, but he saw a message written on the hotel notepad.

His curse filled the room as he read it.

Running back to the door, he scooped up the food bags and set them on the coffee table. Then he exited the room again and went back to the lobby.

"Did you see Ms. Shepherd go out?" he asked the guy behind the desk.

"Yes. She called for a cab."

"How long ago?"

"Twenty minutes."

Twenty minutes was a lifetime.

Mack ran back to the car, jumped inside and started the engine. Lurching out of the parking lot, he headed for the house where they'd visited Jamie's mom.

When he got there, he jumped out of his SUV and ran up the front walk. The door was open.

"Mrs. Wheeler?" he called out.

When nobody answered, he stepped into the house. A thumping noise from the back had him running down the hall, gun drawn.

Gloria Wheeler was sitting in a chair in the bedroom. Gagged and tied.

Chapter Twelve

Blindfolded in the back of the SUV, Jamie struggled to free herself. But it was no good. Her hands were cuffed, and the cuffs were secured to a ring on the side of the luggage compartment in back.

"Please, why are you doing this?"

"You know."

"No, I don't."

"Haven't you figured out that your bastard of a husband started all this when he chased me here? You were supposed to come back to town so I could get you, but you weren't supposed to be investigating the murders. How did you know they had anything to do with me?"

"What murders?"

The man behind the wheel laughed. "Don't play innocent with me. You know all about it, don't you?"

"No."

"You and that detective fellow. Mack Steele. He was a friend of your husband. What are you doing, sleeping with him now?"

She made a muffled sound, and the driver laughed again.

"What do you want with me?"

"You're going to pay. Just like everyone else who helped take my son away from me."

"I never met your son."

"That doesn't matter. You're part of it now. You've been stalking me. "

"I haven't."

"Don't lie," he growled.

The kidnapper pulled to the side of the road and cut the engine. Opening the back door, he stuffed a rag in her mouth and tied it in place. When he spoke again his voice had turned chipper. "Got to take care of something. Be back in a jiffy."

As soon as he'd climbed out of the car and locked the door, Jamie redoubled her frantic efforts to get loose, but it was still impossible. She was stuck here until he released her.

Could she get away then? She hoped so, even when she knew that none of the previous victims had managed it.

She hadn't called him by name when they'd been talking. But she knew who he had to be. He was Henry Fried. He'd killed Craig and three other people. Now he had her. And he knew a lot about her. He'd been at her mother's house, waiting for her.

A sickening thought assaulted her, and she struggled not to moan around the gag. She'd gotten a letter from her mother asking her to come back to town. But Gloria said she hadn't written the letter. Jamie had thought maybe Clark had done it. Now she was pretty sure that it had been Henry Fried, trying to lure her back.

She closed her eyes, clenching and unclenching her fists, wishing she had just waited for a few minutes until Mack had come back with dinner. But Mom had sounded so frantic.

Yesterday, Fried had tried to push her into his SUV. Yes, it must have been him because this was the same vehicle.

After that, Mack had warned her to be careful, but one frantic call had wiped out the warning, and she'd gone charging over to Mom's house. And look where it had gotten her.

But what if she had waited for Mack, like she should have? Maybe that would have been worse. Maybe Fried would have Mack now, too. At least this way, there was some chance that he'd be able to rescue her.

Mack, she mentally called out. *Mack, I'm scared. Please figure out where I am.*

She felt tears stinging the backs of her eyes. There were so many things she should have done differently. And one of them was telling Mack how she felt about him.

She loved him. She'd known that deep down for a long time. But she hadn't been able to cope with it. Instead, she'd pushed him away.

Only if she hadn't done it, they wouldn't have figured out the connection between the victims. For all the good that did her now.

She'd printed that article because she wanted to feel close to Craig. She'd loved him. But that didn't mean she couldn't love again. Have a life again.

She'd turned away from Mack because she'd felt guilty.

Now she might never have a chance to be honest with him.

MACK BOLTED ACROSS THE room and pulled the gag out of Mrs. Wheeler's mouth.

She dragged in air, her eyes wild as she stared at him.

"What happened?" he asked.

"I didn't want anything to happen to Jamie…"

"Jamie," Mack gasped. "Where is she?"

Mrs. Wheeler's eyes pleaded for understanding. "A man

was here. He…" The sentence ended in a scream as a shuffling noise alerted Mack that someone was behind him.

He tried to whirl, but the intruder had already leaped on Mack from behind, throwing him to the floor and banging his head against the hard surface.

Stars danced before his eyes as he tried to regain his senses. Then a fist punched into his back.

Mrs. Wheeler was screaming, "No, stop! You don't understand. It wasn't him."

She continued to scream, as Mack struggled to focus, struggled to free himself. With a tremendous effort, he heaved himself up. The attacker wasn't expecting it, and he tumbled back. Mack leaped on him, landing a punch to his jaw. As his attacker fell to the floor, Mack saw it was Clark Landon.

"What the hell?" Mack choked out as he drew his gun and pointed it at Landon.

"What the hell were you doing to her?" Landon demanded.

"He wasn't doin' nothin'," Mrs. Wheeler shouted. "You're not listening to me. It was another guy."

Mack kept his gun trained on the attacker. "You'd better come clean with me, you bastard. Did you set this up?"

Landon pushed himself up. "What?"

"It wasn't him," Mrs. Wheeler said. "Please, one of you untie me."

Mack backed away and jerked the gun toward Landon. "You untie her." To Mrs. Wheeler, he said, "What happened?"

Landon got to work and Gloria started talking.

"Please believe me, I didn't mean Jamie no harm. A man came to the door. He said he was lookin' for Jamie. I said she wasn't here. He said he'd seen her around town.

Then when I started to close the door on him, he pushed his way in. He tied me up and told me he was going to kill me unless I got Jamie over here. So I called her on her cell phone."

"Where is she?" Mack demanded.

"He took her away."

Mack's curse rang through the room. "That was Henry Fried, the man we've been tracking. The man who killed those women and Jamie's husband."

"Dear God," Mrs. Wheeler wailed.

Mack cursed again, then rounded on Landon. "Are you working with him?"

"I don't know what you're talking about."

"What part did you play in this?"

"I went after Jamie in the parking lot. But that's all. I swear."

"So that *was* you!" Mack growled, fighting a surge of anger. He wanted to bash the bastard in the face, but he knew that would only be counterproductive. Better to keep him talking.

"Yeah, but I swear I didn't do nothing else. I came in here and thought you tied up Gloria."

"Why did you go after Jamie?" he asked in a hard voice.

"Because she had no business coming back here and messin' things up between me and Gloria," Landon answered. "I wanted her to go back to Baltimore where she belongs. I wasn't going to run her over. Honest."

"I hope not." Mack looked from Landon to Jamie's mother. He'd delayed calling the cops. Now he was going to have to do it.

Grim-faced, he pulled out his cell phone and dialed 911.

JAMIE TENSED AS SHE HEARD footsteps heading back toward the car.

"Thanks for waiting," Henry Fried said in a smug voice as he pulled the gag from her mouth.

Jamie didn't bother with a reply. Anything she said might make the situation worse.

He started the engine, then released the emergency brake and started off again.

When she didn't ask where he'd been, he said, "I needed to set something up."

"What?"

"You'll find out soon enough."

He drove, making several turns. Jamie could feel the car going uphill, then down. But that wasn't unusual in Gaptown where few streets were flat.

He slowed and made a sharp turn into a driveway, then pulled forward before getting out again.

Back in the car, he drove into what must be a garage, then cut the engine and opened one of the back doors. She might have lunged toward him, but a cold spray of something hit her in the face. She coughed once, then everything faded to black. The last thing she thought was, *That's how he does it. He drugs them.*

HENRY RUBBED THE PLACE on his neck where Jamie had scratched him the other day. He waiting for several minutes to make sure that she was out cold, although really there should be no doubt. The drug he was using was very reliable. He'd never had a problem before. And he'd developed the delivery system himself so that he could be several feet away when he administered a dose. He'd tried to use it when he'd come to her hotel the other day, but she'd been struggling with him, and he hadn't been able to get the spray out of his pocket.

"Jamie?"

When she didn't answer, he darted forward and poked her hard in the ribs, but she didn't stir. He'd like to scratch her damn neck, but he had a better way to punish her.

Satisfied that it was safe to transfer her to the funhouse, he uncuffed her hands, then picked her up and slung her over his shoulder like a sack of garden soil.

Once he'd bought the stuff by the carload. That was when he'd been a normal guy, with a house and garden. Until Helen had started acting like he was the least important thing in her life, and he'd gotten angry. He'd smacked her around a little, and she'd called the cops on him. Then she'd threatened to take Billy away from him. In a panic he'd bundled his son into the car and started driving…and ended up in this damn town, of all places. With a bunch of people who couldn't mind their own business.

Maybe they hadn't understood the enormity of the crimes they'd committed. But they'd helped Helen take Billy away from him. And he'd never forgiven any of them.

He'd gotten even with the main ones. Now he was going to complete the job. He'd have been satisfied with running Jamie through the funhouse. Then she and Mr. Detective Mack Steele had come to town and started poking their noses in where they didn't belong.

He wanted to know how they'd gotten a line on him. And he was going to find out before he finished them off.

The high fence prevented anyone from seeing what he was doing as he carried Jamie across the yard and through the back door. Then he carried her down to the basement holding cell and dumped her on the bed. After rolling her to her back, he stared down at her. He had her now. The exhibits he'd arranged for her were the last things she'd see on earth.

When she woke up. First, she'd sleep for another couple of hours while he completed the other part of his plan.

WHEN THE 911 OPERATOR answered, Mack clenched the phone in a death grip.

"What is the nature of your emergency?" the woman asked in a controlled voice.

"A woman's been tied up and her daughter abducted."

He went on to give details and Gloria's address. Next he called the Light Street Detective Agency.

Sam Lassiter answered the phone. "Mack, we were wondering when we were going to hear from you."

"Sorry. I thought I could handle this by myself. I found out this morning that the murders here are connected to Craig Shepherd's death."

Sam's exclamation rang through the phone. "What in the hell is going on?"

"It's complicated. Jamie and I came up here because she had a lead on a murder."

"You mean the women found by the side of the road?"

"Yeah." Quickly Mack filled him in. "I've called the cops," he added. "But the bastard's got Jamie. And I don't know how long he holds his victims before he kills them. We've got to find her. Can you start looking through property records? He could be using a vacant house. He could have rented a property. Or he could even have bought something."

"Okay. We'll get back to you stat."

As soon as he hung up, the phone rang again.

"Mack Steele."

"If you want to see your little slut again, you'll follow my directions."

"Who is this?"

"I think you have a good idea."

He gripped the phone, wondering what to say.

"Did you call the cops?"

"Yes."

"That was a mistake."

When he didn't reply, the man said, "Better get out of there before they arrive. I want you to meet me at the corner of Mountain and Walnut. There's an abandoned gas station on the corner. Pull around back. And if you're thinking of asking the cops to meet you there, don't. Because that's the way to get Jamie Shepherd killed. So get going."

Mack pressed the off button and turned to Mrs. Wheeler. "The cops will be here soon."

"You're not leaving, are you?"

"I've got to.

"You heard what I told the detective agency. When the police get here, tell them what happened. Tell them the man who has Jamie called me and asked me to meet him at the gas station at the corner of Mountain and Walnut. The man is named Henry Fried. He was convicted of kidnapping his son. He murdered the two women whose bodies were dumped this week. They both had contact with Fried's son. Got all that?"

He turned and charged out the door.

After jerking the SUV from the curb, he clicked his cell phone again and made another call to Light Street.

Sam answered again. "You got any additional information?" he asked.

"The killer just called me. He asked me to meet him at an abandoned gas station."

"Not a good idea."

"I know. But I don't have any choice, do I? He said that if I don't meet him, he's going to kill Jamie."

"And you, too, likely," Sam said bluntly.

He knew Sam was right. "I told Jamie's mom and her boyfriend to tell the cops everything they know. My notes on the case are on my computer files."

"Hunter and Brady are already on their way. They're coming by chopper. You can talk to them soon."

Hunter Kelley and Brady Lockwood, two of Light Street's best men.

"Thanks," he answered. "Meanwhile, you can get started on the research end. The information's in a file called Gaptown. You can download it, and you'll have almost everything I know. That and the information from Jamie's mom."

"Will do. But I wish you could hold off on the gas station thing until Hunter and Brady arrive."

Mack sighed. "That would make sense from a tactical point of view. Except that by then it will be too late. Jamie's got to be my first priority."

"It's probably a trap."

"I know. I'll be careful."

"What do you want us to do if you're out of commission by the time we get to Gaptown?" Sam asked.

"That's a nice way to put it."

"Just trying to be realistic."

"I guess you add me to the search list."

He clicked off, knowing that he was taking a chance, but he simply couldn't proceed any other way.

Jamie's life was at stake.

HENRY WALKED TO A HIDDEN door and stepped through to a flight of stairs that led to the first floor. Too bad he'd had to make such drastic alterations in this grand old house. But somebody else could pay for the restoration job later.

If he'd wanted to stay here, he could have done the reno himself. Ironically, he'd acquired plenty of money while he was in prison. At first he'd sat around being angry with Helen and all the other people who had taken his son away. Then he'd decided that was getting him nowhere. Instead, he'd turned his attention back to some of the inventions he'd been perfecting when his bitch of a wife had run away with his son.

He couldn't work with actual models, but he had a good mind for abstract thinking. He'd contacted a firm that was interested in his ideas for modifications to standard telephones. They'd bought some of his plans for a good price. Through his lawyer, he'd invested the money and done well, partly by pulling out of the market at the right time.

He climbed the stairs to the second floor of the house, where he'd fixed himself a comfortable media room so he could relax while he waited for his victims to wake up. He liked the contrast. They were on a hard bunk in a cold, musty basement cell. He was up here with all the comforts of home.

After stepping inside and closing the door, he checked his watch. Plenty of time before the show began. Humming softly to himself, he opened the small refrigerator he'd installed for convenience and got out a soft drink. After taking a couple of sips, he settled himself in a comfortable easy chair.

The routine was soothing. It allowed him to forget about his anger for a while. He was almost done with this phase of his life. After he'd taken his revenge, he was going to use his money for another purpose—to find his son.

He'd let Helen get comfortable. Probably she thought he was never going to find her, and she was safe. Which meant she'd probably let down her guard, and she wouldn't be so hard to find.

He'd kill her in a way that would look like an accident. He'd spent a lot of time thinking about what that would be exactly. Maybe a hit and run, like with Craig Shepherd. Only he'd have to make sure Billy wasn't with her.

Then he'd show up, the concerned father come to rescue his child. He'd take Billy away, and the two of them could live together. He hoped Helen hadn't said too much about him. Probably she hadn't because she didn't want him to be a bad influence on the boy. But even if she'd blabbed about him every day, he'd get back that special relationship he and Billy had once had. He knew he could do it.

As he sipped his drink, he looked at the bank of monitors on the opposite wall. Some showed the hallways of the funhouse. One showed Jamie's cell.

He watched her sleeping, then switched to a camera at a remote site, the back parking lot of the gas station.

Settling back in his chair, he waited for Mack Steele to show up.

Would the guy take a chance on declining the invitation? Henry thought not. He was betting that Steele would come because he didn't want to be responsible for getting Jamie Shepherd killed.

Not yet, anyway.

PRAYING THAT IT WASN'T too late, Mack headed for the meeting place, trying not to speed since he didn't want to get stopped by the cops and have to come up with an explanation.

He slowed as he approached the corner, which was in a seedy part of town where a lot of the businesses were closed. He drove slowly past the service station, wondering what Fried expected—and what he should expect from Fried.

Probably the guy thought he'd arrive by car. Instead, Mack parked down the block and walked cautiously toward the empty parking lot of the station.

The windows were boarded up and the pumps were gone. So where was Fried hiding? Or was he across the street?

Mack turned to scan the other side of the street. He saw a row of low commercial buildings. One had been a flower shop, another an insurance agency. There were lights in the window of a beauty parlor, but he didn't see anyone inside. Nor did he see any cars. Had Fried come on foot, too?

Fear leaped inside him as a new thought surfaced. Was this all just a distraction so that Fried could finish off Jamie without interference?

Mack wanted to dash into the parking lot and find Fried. But he wasn't a complete fool. He knew this could be some kind of trap.

The gas station was separated from the next property by a six-foot-high wooden board fence.

Instead of heading straight there, Mack walked quietly along the other side of the fence. When he was far enough from the street, he climbed into the low branches of a tree and looked over at the vacant establishment.

It was evening now, and he probed the shadows, wishing he had night-vision goggles. But he hadn't considered that kind of equipment when he'd planned his trip to Gaptown.

He climbed farther into the tree, then along a branch that hung over the fence. When he was on the other side, he eased down to the oil-stained parking lot. Again he waited, wondering when Fried would show up.

Mack had crossed about six feet of concrete, heading for the back of the station when he thought he heard a door open.

He went still, turning quietly toward the sound, and saw that the men's room door was now flapping back and forth. It shouldn't be unlocked. Not when anybody could walk right in and vandalize the place.

Unsure of what to do, he stopped short, listening.

Maybe this wasn't such a great idea, after all. Maybe he should have waited for the Light Street men. But he hadn't been able to do it. Not when Fried had threatened Jamie's life.

Mack heard nothing. After long moments, he took a step closer, then another.

"Fried?" he called out.

Nobody answered.

"Jamie?" he tried, hoping against hope that somehow she was in there.

Again, nothing.

What the hell was the guy up to? Had Fried done something to the door, or had it come unlatched on its own?

Not likely. This was a setup, all right. But suppose Jamie was in there?

He'd almost reached the door when a stream of vapor shot from inside the little room.

Mack's reflexes were good. He jumped instantly back, but it was a split-second too late. His head began to spin, and he dropped to the hard concrete as the lights went out around him.

Chapter Thirteen

Henry drove slowly up the block toward the gas station. He hadn't wanted to risk being there in person when the smart-ass detective arrived. Better to stay safe until his special equipment had done its work.

Still, he approached with caution. No use taking any unnecessary chances.

He spotted the guy's car down the block and laughed. Fat lot of good that tricky move had done him.

At the darkened property, he opened his window and shined a powerful light into the parking area, where he saw Steele lying on the ground. He was near the door to the men's room, and he wasn't moving. The same place where Henry had last seen him on the TV monitor. There hadn't been any sound, but the picture had told the story.

He gunned the engine of the SUV and plowed forward. He could have run over the guy, but what fun would that be? Just another dead detective lying on the pavement. No entertainment value in that. Like with Craig Shepherd. He'd have taken Shepherd to the funhouse, if he'd been able to, but the place hadn't been finished yet. He'd opted to get Shepherd out of the way before he could start messing around in the case again. Too bad his wife and Steele had picked it up again. What were they doing, he thought, checking out Shepherd's old cases?

After waiting several moments, he got out of his car and approached the man sprawled on the pavement.

Anyone awake would have jumped up and gotten out of the way when he heard the car bearing down on him. Steele hadn't moved.

Henry walked over and kicked the guy in the ribs. He didn't respond. Apparently he'd hit his head when he went down. It was still bleeding.

Too bad for him.

He kept staring at the guy, knowing they'd met before. At that rib and crabcake restaurant. He hadn't realized at the time who it was. But when he'd gone back over Jamie's contacts, he'd seen Steele's photo.

Well, he had the bastard now.

The booby trap at the gas station had worked perfectly, the way he'd known it would. Every piece of equipment he designed worked perfectly. And there was no need to worry about somebody stumbling in here. He'd rigged some spooky effects in this parking lot. Like ghostly rattlings and moans at random times. There weren't many people who'd risk coming in here after dark.

JAMIE WOKE WITH A pounding headache. Where was she?

Not in the hotel room where she'd been with Mack. She was lying on a narrow cot in a dank, windowless room. Above her a dull light shone from a bulb shielded by a wire cage.

When she sat up, she had to fight a wave of nausea. Even as she grappled with her body's reaction, horrible memories assaulted her.

Mom had called. She'd rushed over there, and then she'd burst in and found her mother tied up in the bedroom.

She gasped, as the past few hours rushed back.

He had her. Fried. The killer. He'd tricked her into going to her mother's, and he'd ordered her out of the house at gunpoint. Then he must have taken her here.

To the funhouse. She knew that was where she had to be.

She wanted to scream, but she thought he might be watching her, and she wasn't going to give him the satisfaction of knowing she was terrified.

Cautiously, she let her gaze search the room and found the camera high up on the wall. When she looked down, she saw something on the ground just inside the door. At first she couldn't figure out what it was.

Then she gasped.

"Mack."

He was curled in a heap at the other side of the cell, and he didn't move when she called his name.

Her heart in her throat, she heaved herself off the bed and wavered on unsteady legs toward him.

FROM HIS COMFORTABLE REFUGE, Henry watched the tender scene in the basement cell. Maybe Jamie Shepherd thought her boyfriend was dead. She'd find out soon enough that he was only damaged.

He watched her push off the bed and stagger across the room. She was just a woman. Weak like all women. But there was something about her that made him nervous. He kept thinking that he'd seen her in some unexpected context. Not in the restaurant with Steele. She hadn't been there.

But where?

He shuddered. It wasn't just that he'd seen her. He couldn't shake the conviction that she'd been watching him.

But that was impossible. He hadn't had any previous

personal contact with her except the time he'd tried to shove her into the SUV. She'd gotten away then, but he had her now, and he wasn't going to let any strange thoughts interfere with his enjoyment of this drama.

This was the final act. As soon as the man and woman down there in the cell were dead, he'd clear out of Gaptown and start looking for his son. Maybe he wouldn't even take the time to dump the bodies. He could just leave them here to rot until someone came into the house.

Yeah, maybe that was the best thing to do at this stage of the game. Probably the cops were crawling all over town by now. Of course, they'd never find this place in time. It was too well hidden—in plain sight. But he'd better not press his luck.

His gaze flicked back to the woman, trying to figure out where he'd seen her before. He shook his head, as a logical explanation came to him. He'd studied her picture like he'd studied Steele's. He knew exactly who she was. That was why she looked so familiar.

The explanation made sense. But he'd had plenty of pictures of the other victims, too, and he didn't have the same spooky feeling about them.

JAMIE KNELT ON THE floor.

"Mack," she said again in a broken voice. She'd thought that maybe he could rescue her. Apparently he'd come looking for her and ended up in the same cell with her.

He was lying on his back, and she saw that blood had caked in his hair. Either he'd hit his head, or Fried had hit him with something.

"Mack. Are you all right, Mack?" she cried.

He made a moaning sound and stirred.

Remembering where the camera was, she leaned over him, blocking Fried's view of them.

"Mack, wake up," she whispered. "But don't let him know you're awake. I'm between you and the camera, so he can't see your face. Okay?"

She waited for long, tense moments.

His eyes blinked open, and he stared up at her. When he started to speak, she pressed her fingers to his mouth. "Don't let him know you're awake," she whispered again.

"Okay," he answered in a barely audible voice.

She reached for his hand and meshed her fingers with his. For long moments, neither of them spoke. Then his face took on a mixture of anger and regret. "I got caught."

"What happened?"

"He called and said he'd kill you if I didn't meet him. So I went to the gas station where I thought he was waiting. He'd booby-trapped the place."

She sucked in a sharp breath and whispered, "I'm sorry."

"Not your fault."

Gingerly, she touched his forehead. "You're bleeding."

"I fell on my face when the gas hit me."

"I'm sorry," she said again. "I shouldn't have rushed over to my mom's."

Sitting up straighter, she looked around the room. There was a sink and a toilet in one corner, and a rack with a towel.

"I'm going to wash your forehead," she whispered.

Scrambling up, she went to the sink and wet the towel, then returned to Mack where she blocked the view of the camera again and washed the blood off his forehead.

"I guess I look like hell," Mack said in a low voice.

"Yeah."

"Come closer."

When she bent over him, he whispered, "The police are on the case. Also the Light Street men."

"Okay," she mouthed, wondering if any of that would help.

Before she could say anything else, a voice boomed from a hidden speaker. "I know you're awake, Steele. If you keep playing possum, you could end up dead for real."

Neither of them moved.

"I'll give you a chance to get out of here. All you have to do is find the right door."

"He's lying," Jamie mouthed.

Mack answered with a small nod, then winced, and she knew it must hurt his head to move it.

The door clicked.

"Go out and explore your new environment," Fried's voice boomed. "It's a funhouse. Like for Halloween."

"A funhouse," Jamie murmured, like she didn't already know. "What if we don't go out there?"

"Then I'll flood the room with tear gas. You'll have to leave, and you won't be in such good shape to appreciate the games I've prepared for you."

Mack heaved himself up, staggering a little and grabbing the wall to steady himself.

"I'm not so good on my feet," he called out.

"Too bad."

"Give me a minute. I need a drink of water."

"Why should I let you?"

"Because it won't be as much fun running me through your maze like a lab rat if I'm half dead."

IT WAS DAWN WHEN the helicopter landed in a field outside of town. Sam had called ahead and arranged for a car to meet Hunter and Brady, and also the additional agents who were on their way.

When the two lean, dark-haired men climbed out of the chopper, their ride was waiting for them.

"Thanks for the quick service," Brady said as he paid the driver.

"When will the other chopper arrive?"

"They're about twenty minutes behind us with Jed Prentiss and Max Dakota."

"We'll be waiting."

As soon as they roared away, Hunter got out his cell phone and computer and dialed Mack's number. There was no answer.

He looked at Brady. "Bad news. Mack's off the air."

"We'll start at his last known location. The gas station."

While they drove, Hunter called Sam Lassiter back at the office.

"What have you got for me?" he asked.

"I have the location of properties that have been sold or rented in the past twelve months."

"You think that's far enough back?" Hunter asked.

"I hope so. The list should already be in your inbox."

As Brady drove toward town, Hunter accessed his mail.

"According to Mack's notes, the house is most likely in an isolated location."

"Okay, we'll get that information to the police," Brady said as they drove slowly toward the gas station. On the street half a block away, they found Mack's car. It was empty.

After checking it out, they cautiously approached his last known location. The parking lot was also empty, but near the open door to the men's room, they found a small pool of blood.

Brady cursed as they cautiously approached the open door.

Inside was a some kind of mechanism that looked like it was designed to spray gas at someone outside the door.

Brady cursed again. "I guess that's how the bastard nailed him."

Hunter looked at the blood. "Did he shoot him?"

"No way of knowing. He could have hit his head when he went down."

"We've got to assume Fried's got him and Jamie."

JAMIE WAITED FOR THE answer with her breath shallow.

"True," their captor answered. "You can have a few more minutes in your cell."

Mack gave her a victorious look. It wasn't much of a victory, but it bought them a little time, and it proved that Fried wanted a certain kind of experience.

Mack kept his hand on the wall as he moved to the sink, and she watched him with anxiety. He looked like he could barely walk, but maybe he was putting on a show for Fried, so he'd think it would be easy to come down into the funhouse to finish off his victims.

She shuddered. That wasn't going to happen to her and Mack. There were two of them, and only one of him.

Still, she knew from the way she'd been handled that Fried was a man who hated to take chances. He'd make sure the odds were tipped in his favor.

She watched Mack check his pockets and find that they were all empty.

Of course Fried wouldn't allow him to keep anything like a cell phone that could help him.

When he'd finished searching, he cupped his hands

under the faucet and lifted them to his lips, repeating the process several times. Then he splashed cold water on his face and shook his head.

"You, too," he said. "Take a drink."

She also drank, then looked at Mack. She wanted to talk to him, but if she did, Fried would hear her. She wanted to remind him that she knew this place better than their captor could imagine. That had to give her an advantage, she hoped.

"Better get going," the voice boomed.

WITH NO OTHER OPTIONS, Brady and Hunter started checking properties around the Gaptown area. The first ten were too small.

Then they found a large house that looked like it could fit the description.

But as they drew closer, Brady's eyes narrowed. Although it was still early in the morning, a boy and girl who appeared to be about three or four were riding tricycles up and down the driveway. Another three children were playing on a jungle gym. And two women were giving the two men in the car long looks.

After a quick conversation, one of them walked toward the vehicle but stopped a few yards away.

"Can I help you?" she asked, eyeing them with suspicion. Which was the right thing to do when a couple of strange men were hanging around a house with a bunch of kids.

"We were looking for a man who bought a large, old house in the Gaptown area," he said, knowing the explanation sounded lame.

"Well, this is the Kiddy Care Day Care Center," the woman said.

"And you purchased this house within the past year?" Brady asked.

"Listen, mister, if you don't leave here right away, I'm going to call the police."

"Sorry, ma'am," Brady said.

Hunter pulled away, and they drove to the end of the street and made a U-turn.

"This is going to take some time," Brady muttered.

MACK TOOK JAMIE'S HAND and squeezed, hoping he could reassure her with his touch.

He was still cursing himself for getting caught as they walked through the door and into a dimly-lit basement corridor that smelled like a graveyard. What had Fried done, stuffed dead rats in the walls?

So this was what the place was like. Jamie had described the funhouse, but he hadn't gotten the complete picture until now. He could see that one side of the hallway was probably formed from the original wall of the house. The other had been constructed of plywood.

He kicked at it, testing how well built it was, and it flexed a little.

On the walls were color posters from old horror movies. *Night of the Living Dead. The Texas Chainsaw Massacre. Nightmare on Elm Street.* Gruesome, but tame compared to what Jamie had told him was in the rest of the house.

As soon as they were out of the cell, he heard the lock click behind them. No going back that way, he thought.

Suddenly slasher movie music blared from hidden speakers. Beside him, Jamie shivered and he turned to her and pulled her into his arms, holding her tight.

She clung to him just as tightly.

He brought his mouth to her ear and spoke in a low voice. "I'm sorry."

"You didn't do anything."

"I got caught."

"So did I." She swallowed hard.

"But I should have been prepared for something tricky at the gas station."

"Don't! You didn't know what to expect."

He dragged in a breath, telling himself there was no point in focusing on what they should have done. The only important thing was what they did now.

"He thinks he's going to win, but we'll get out of this together," he told her, hoping to hell it was true.

She nodded against his shoulder, but he wasn't sure she believed him.

She raised her face and looked at him in the dim light. "Just in case," she said, then stopped as her voice broke.

"Steady," he murmured.

She nodded. "I'm okay."

He knew it had to be a lie, but he only nodded.

"Just in case we don't get out of here, I want you to know something important. I love you."

Despite everything, happiness swelled inside him. "Oh, Jamie. I love you, too. So much. I've ached to tell you, but I was afraid to say it. Afraid that the words would send you running as fast as you could in the other direction."

"I might have run," she admitted. "But now I've got my head screwed on straight. Funny how looming death sorts out your priorities."

"This isn't the end for us," he said fiercely. "I promise."

She closed her eyes, and he knew she was trying to block out this horrible place as she pulled his mouth down to hers for a long, passionate kiss. He clung to her, his lips moving over hers, praying that it wasn't for the last time.

"Just so you know what you have to look forward to,"

she said when they came up for air. Then she brought her mouth to his ear and spoke in a barely audible whisper.

"We've got an advantage. Remember, I've been here before. I know how this place works. I think I can avoid the worst traps. I hope," she added.

They were still standing by the door. From within the cell, Mack heard a hissing noise. Then noxious gas began to seep around the cracks in the door, and they both began to cough.

Mack grabbed her hand, and they staggered down the hall, still coughing. They turned a corner and stopped, both of them wheezing.

"We should get out of this hallway," he muttered.

Still clasping her hand, he led her farther away from the cell. Before they'd gotten more than ten paces, an explosion rocked the corridor.

Mack threw Jamie to the floor, coming down on top of her to protect her from the blast.

In the confined space, his ears were ringing and he braced to feel chunks of cement or cinder block raining down on his back and head. But it didn't happen.

Only smoke and dust filled the air.

"It's not real." As she spoke, the words set off a coughing fit.

He eased off of her, and they both sat up and looked around. As the dust settled, they could see a blackened place on the floor where some kind of small explosive had detonated, creating the illusion of something worse.

"Just one of his little tricks," she managed to choke out.

"Yeah."

Mack leaned his head against the wall, struggling for breath, trying his damnedest not to pass out.

"I'll bet he's watching us and laughing," she murmured, looking up, trying to spot a hidden camera.

He probably had cameras at the gas station, too, Mack thought, and he'd watched Mack fall into his trap. He wanted to fill the air with curses, but he held the words back.

Jamie started to speak again but stopped herself, and he guessed she'd thought of some information she didn't want the bastard to know.

Getting to her knees, she put her mouth to his ear. "I didn't see anything like this when I was here before."

"He probably rotates his tricks," he muttered.

He'd been hoping Jamie could figure out how to escape. Now he realized he'd been fooling himself.

Chapter Fourteen

Henry got up and paced across his lounge area, turning his head so he could keep the TV monitor in his line of vision.

The bastards were talking about something, and they didn't want him to hear them. Did that mean they realized the entire funhouse was wired for sound and not just the basement cell?

How could they know about that?

Maybe the detective had simply warned her to be cautious.

He turned off the background music and tried jacking up the volume control, but he still couldn't pick up their conversation.

He cursed loudly. He had the feeling they were planning something. That wasn't going to do them any good. They couldn't hide. They couldn't get out of the house. What did they think they could do that they were trying to keep him from knowing about?

Maybe he should end this game more quickly than he'd planned. That would eliminate any threat. But it would also eliminate a great deal of his enjoyment.

He studied the screen again, then zoomed in on the couple. The guy looked like he was in pretty bad shape. Maybe there was no need to rush, after all.

"IF WE STAY HERE, are we going to get gassed or something?" Mack muttered.

"I don't know." Again she put her mouth to his ear. "If we can get to the next floor, we should head for the dining room. From there we can get to the front door. Then we can use one of the dining room chairs to batter through a window."

He turned his head to reverse their positions. "Are there other exits?"

"There have to be."

"Did you see any others?"

"No."

"We'll find one." He stayed where he was, leaning against the wall and gathering his strength. Another idea was forming in his mind. It might not do them a damn bit of good, but they wouldn't know until they tried.

Again he spoke in a whisper. "I'm willing to bet that Fried is somewhere in the house. He thinks we can't get to him, but maybe we can."

"Where would he be?" Jamie asked in a low voice.

"You said the funhouse is on the first floor and in the basement, so he'd probably be on the next level."

"I saw stairs going up from the front hall," she recalled. "I bet he didn't think anyone would get into the foyer, but that's where I landed in my last dream."

"Right."

Jamie nodded. "We should go," she said. "Before he does something else to us."

Mack heaved himself to his feet.

She gave him a critical look. "How are you?"

"Fine."

She made a snorting sound. "Sure."

Down the hallway, they came to a place where they had to go right or left. Jamie had talked about choices like this.

It could be bad either way. But they hadn't been playing Fried's game very long. He wouldn't have a fatal trap so soon in the game, would he?

Mack hoped not. As they walked slowly forward, he kept thinking about how this bastard's game must work. He was watching them now on a TV monitor, but he couldn't be watching all the time. Sooner or later he was going to come down here to get them. Then they'd be out of sight— at least for a little while. With any luck that would give them time to turn the tables and set some kind of trap for the guy.

He scrambled for information, wishing he'd paid more attention to Jamie's descriptions of the traps in here, but at first he hadn't thought it was real. And he certainly hadn't thought he'd end up in this hellhole.

HUNTER HAD SWITCHED ON the reading light and was scanning the list of houses that had been purchased or rented in the past twelve months. Jed and Max had also arrived, and they were checking out property on the east side of town.

Hunter kept scanning the list as Brady drove to the next west side location. This time when they reached the property, they found that a bulldozer had flattened the structure. Apparently someone had bought the house for the purpose of tearing it down and using the land.

Another dead end.

Brady turned the car around. "There's got to be a better way to do this."

Hunter looked up from the list. "I've been thinking. Last summer, Kathryn and I took Ethan to Gaptown. There's a state park up here with an artificial lake. We had a fun time there, but we also went into town for some meals and to shop. There are a lot of mansions in the West End.

Apparently they're scooped up by doctors and lawyers and other people with money. Some live there all year round. Others just use them for vacation houses. He could be using one of those."

Brady considered the theory. "But if someone bought a big mansion in an upscale neighborhood, wouldn't the neighbors pay attention to the property transfer?"

Hunter shrugged. "They might. But if it's one of those owners who's just in town off and on, the neighbors might not get to know him." He pointed to the list. "There's a house on Washington Street that I think we should investigate."

"Why?"

"The guy who bought it is named Mr. Hyde."

Brady shook his head. "Could be a coincidence."

"Or our guy thinking he's tricky."

MACK LEANED TOWARD JAMIE and spoke into her ear again. "We'd better try to get upstairs."

She thought for a moment. "I remember there's a big room somewhere down here. It's got a flight of steps going up."

"Okay."

He stopped, taking a moment to test his arms and legs. He wasn't up to par, but he was feeling better than when he'd first awakened on the cold cellar floor.

Still speaking into Jamie's ear, he asked, "Do you know which way?"

She gave him a sick look. "I wish I did."

"We'll find it together," he said, taking her hand and starting down the corridor toward the right.

They'd walked a yard when the cement floor changed to plywood.

Thirty seconds after they'd stepped onto it, the surface began to roll and shake.

Mack's curse rang through the hallway as he looked over his shoulder.

"Too far to go back," he muttered. "Keep going."

The motion accelerated, tumbling them back and forth.

"Get down," he shouted to Jamie.

She dropped to the floor and braced her hands against the rocking floor.

In the dim light, he could see that the shaking stopped a couple of yards from where they were being bounced around.

"Crawl," he muttered as he steadied himself on hands and knees and began moving across the tipping surface. When the motion became even more violent, he feared they'd break an arm or leg.

Their progress was slow, but he finally clambered off onto solid floor, then turned to help Jamie off.

As soon as they'd cleared the plywood floor, it stopped rocking. Either Fried was watching them and had turned off the effect, or there were sensors in the floor to tell the mechanism that the weight of their bodies was now absent. He'd like to know which.

Although he was on solid ground, his head kept spinning, and he leaned against the wall, fighting nausea.

Jamie crawled toward him and laid her head against his shoulder.

"That was sure a fun ride," she muttered.

He snorted. "Oh yeah."

They sat for several moments until he noticed something changing. The floor had been cold. Now it was becoming uncomfortably hot.

Jamie looked at him in alarm. "What's happening?"

"Looks like we're on the hot seat. Better get moving."

BACK IN TOWN, BRADY TURNED onto Washington Street, marveling at the rows of grand old houses that had been restored to their glory days.

"These babies would be worth millions in Baltimore," he said.

"But up here, you can probably scoop them up much cheaper. Especially since the recession hit," Hunter answered, then pointed toward a sprawling gray Victorian with a tower at the front entrance. A high wooden fence enclosed the back yard. "That's the one."

He spotted a man watching them from a nearby driveway and pulled to a stop. Rolling down his window, he pointed to the Victorian and said, "We were looking for property to buy up here. That place is exactly what we want. You don't know if it's for sale, do you?"

"Probably not. It changed hands recently."

"Does the owner work at the hospital?"

"Naw. I think he's one of the carpetbaggers who come in here and pick up prime real estate. He's been in and out, fixing it up, but I don't think he actually lives there. Maybe he's going to flip it."

"If he's going to flip it, we should talk to him."

"He's not real friendly."

"Have you seen the inside?"

"He hasn't invited the neighbors in."

"Has he been here recently?"

The man thought for a moment. "He was around late last night. Then he left and came in again this morning."

"Okay, thanks."

Brady rolled up the window and pulled away. "That would match the time frame when he captured Jamie and Mack."

He came to a narrow side street and took it. The street curved around in back of the row of houses, which turned out to be built on the side of a steep hill. He stopped in back of the house next to the Victorian.

"You think that could be the funhouse?" Hunter asked.

"Well, Hyde bought it eight months ago. He's fixing the place up, which could mean either restoring the interior or making it into his private amusement park. He's got a tricky name, and his movements fit the abductions…but all that could be perfectly innocent. We sure don't have enough evidence for a home invasion."

Brady shook his head and continued. "If it is him, he could have sensors and cameras around the house to make sure nobody's sneaking up on him. If Jamie and Mack are in there, we've got to figure out how to help them without getting them killed."

MACK SPOKE INTO JAMIE'S ear again. "I think it's time to give the tricky little bastard a big surprise."

He stood up in the narrow corridor and braced his shoulders against the old brick basement wall of the house. Then he rammed his foot into the opposite plywood wall.

Jamie saw it waver. It wasn't as solid as it looked.

She wasn't as strong as Mack, but she also braced her shoulder against the wall and helped him kick, feeling the wall give.

They both kept kicking and bashing, and she heard a tearing sound as the structure gave way and fell forward, crashing to the floor. When it stopped reverberating, they were facing a large empty room.

"This is the room I saw in my second trip to the house," Jamie whispered, trying not to give her excitement away. She pointed to the other side of the space. "And there are the stairs."

"We've got to get across," Mack said.

She thought back to what she'd seen in her dream. "When we do, something will come down and attack us," she murmured.

"I think we've got a partial solution." Mack bent to the plywood that he'd kicked to the floor. "We can hold this over our heads for a shield as we cross the room."

UPSTAIRS IN HIS LOUNGE, Henry exploded in anger. He'd settled down for a satisfying game, but those bastards were wrecking his funhouse. They weren't supposed to break the place up. They were supposed to play by his rules. Run down the corridors. Try to get out. Shriek when they got caught in one of his traps.

But they weren't doing any of that now. Damn them! He'd wanted to question them before they died. Maybe he wouldn't have time for that now.

Jumping up, he ran to the bank of computers along the wall. He hadn't planned to finish them off yet, but it looked like he was going to have to do it now before things got any more out of control.

He pulled a lever, sending a spray of acid down from the ceiling of the basement room.

"OH LORD, WHAT'S THAT?" Jamie gasped, coughing as she and Mack huddled under the plywood, holding it above them as they crossed the room.

"Acid," Mack gasped out. "Hurry before the floor gets covered."

They made it across the room and onto the stairs. Looking back, she saw pools of liquid puddling on the floor, where it sizzled, sending a caustic vapor wafting up toward them.

They were both coughing as they climbed the stairs, tears blurring Jamie's vision.

Mack kept the shield over them, tipping it to make any liquid that hit the plywood run off toward the basement floor as he and Jamie clambered up the stairs, trying to get out of the room as fast as they could.

There was a door at the top, and it wasn't locked, probably because Fried hadn't planned to use the acid. Which meant he must be getting desperate.

A desperate man might try something else swift and deadly, Mack knew. Or he might make a bad mistake.

Mack eased part way through the opening, reaching out his arms to hold the plywood for Jamie, who followed as quickly as she could. When she had tumbled into the hallway, he threw the plywood down the stairs, where it splashed onto the floor, sending up an acid spray that made them jump back.

They sat, panting, in the corridor. When noxious fumes drifted up toward them, setting off another coughing fit, Mack slammed the door.

"I never saw anything like that before," he said.

"It means finishing us off is more important than the game."

Leaning close to Jamie, he whispered, "Can you find the dining room?"

"Give me a minute. My eyes are stinging." She swiped her sleeve over her face, wondering if they were going to make it out of here alive. What else did Fried have planned?

ON THE FLOOR ABOVE, Henry jumped up and down, beside himself with anger. He'd thought for sure he would get them with the deadly shower in the large basement room, but they had made it to the first floor.

Although he was certain he had them trapped, he

couldn't take a chance on anything now. He would have to go down there himself and end the game.

For the first time, he felt a sizzle of uncertainty. All along he'd had the upper hand with his victims, but Shepherd and Steele were not like anyone else he'd run through his maze.

They seemed to have an uncanny ability to avoid the traps he'd set. Like that plywood shield. It was almost as if they were expecting something to come down from the ceiling.

What the hell was going on? They couldn't know. Could they?

Still cursing, he watched the action below, judging the right moment to personally take command of the playing field.

At the end of the game, he'd always gone after the victims in the funhouse up close and personal, with knives. That way, he had the satisfaction of plunging the blade into their flesh.

With these two hard cases he wasn't going to take a chance on getting close enough for hand work. Better safe than sorry, he told himself. From a drawer in the wall unit, he pulled out a Sig Sauer and made sure the safety was off.

Then he flipped a series of switches on the control panel so that the final drama would play out the way he wanted.

When he was ready to leave his lounge, he looked at the monitors one last time to check their location before stepping into the hall.

JAMIE GLANCED AROUND, TRYING to orient herself, then gasped as she realized their position. "I've got a better idea.

If we go that way, we'll hit the front hall." She pointed down the corridor.

Mack nodded, and followed her to the right. They came to a door that was locked, but Mack kicked it in and they plowed through into the foyer.

"Thank God."

He dashed to the front door. It was secured with two locks, one a dead bolt that required a key. There were long, narrow windows on either side of the door, but they were sealed with plywood.

This time when he used his foot to try and bash through, there was no effect.

"We need something to use as a battering ram," he muttered.

"I guess we go in the dining room after all. We can use one of the chairs."

Jamie was already heading for the door that she'd used in her dream. It was locked, and it was solid. Too heavy for Mack to break down.

"Other way," she shouted, heading for the hallway.

Before she'd gotten more than a few feet down the corridor, something shot down from the ceiling.

It was a feathered monster. A great black bird whose bill clanked with stainless-steel knives. As it came swooping down at them, she saw needle-sharp claws. Mack was looking the other way, and the thing was heading straight at him.

Chapter Fifteen

As the bird shot toward Mack, she shouted "Watch out," and leaped toward him, pushing him out of the way and rolling as she hit the floor.

Mack hit the ground, dodging the talons, but one of them caught his sleeve and scraped across his arm.

Jamie gasped as she saw a line of blood.

"You're hurt."

"It's nothing."

He was just pushing himself up when a popping sound filled the air. Mack grabbed her by the shoulder, pulling her across the floor and farther into the hallway.

"What was that?" she gasped.

"He's got a gun."

"He never did before."

"Yeah, well, you didn't mention acid before, either. I guess he doesn't like the way we're getting out of his traps. He's still on the stairs. Can we get to the dining room?"

Jamie took a moment to orient herself. "Yes," she finally said, pointing to the right and praying that she hadn't gotten twisted around.

She moved cautiously down the hall with Mack right behind her. "Stay away from the right-hand wall," she told him. "There's a trapdoor somewhere along there."

They hurried along the left side of the hallway, through the next doorway and into the dining room.

"Watch out for a spider," she told Mack.

To trigger the mechanism, she waved her arm through the doorway, and the thing zoomed down. When it had landed on the table, she stepped into the room, glad that Fried hadn't activated the flashing lights.

Orienting herself, she pointed to another door at the far end of the room.

"That's the exit that leads back to the front hall," she said, thinking that Fried wasn't going to hear her on his microphone. He was already down on this level. With a gun.

She glanced at Mack. "Is he out there? Or is he circling around, do you think?"

"Don't know."

"Careful of the chairs. They may pull out by themselves and hit you."

Mack kicked out a leg, making one of the chairs shoot away from the table. He avoided it and yanked another out of position, looking at the seats and seeing the knives that she'd told him about.

He worked to pull two knives loose, handing one to her and sticking the other in his waistband. Then he started moving the chairs, laying one across each doorway, a little inside the room.

"What can I do?"

"Can you bash out the lights?"

She reached for the candelabra in the middle of the table. It was sticky with artificial spider webs, but she grasped it firmly, swinging it at the chandelier, shattering the bulbs.

A noise in the hallway made her go rigid.

"Under the table," Mack whispered.

She dived below the table, just as another shot rang out.

"Got ya."

Obviously confident that he had them cornered, Fried came charging into the room. In the darkness, he didn't see the chair in his path and pitched forward, cursing as he came down on the carpet.

Mack was on him in an instant, striking at him in the back of the neck with the knife.

Jamie sprang forward, her own knife in her hand. Without any hesitation, she chopped down at the killer, hitting him in the back, wincing as she heard the blade clash against bone.

Fried lay sprawled across the chair. Mack pulled the gun out of his hand and turned him over, then yanked off his death mask. He sucked in a sharp breath when he saw the man's face.

"What is it, Mack?"

"He was in the restaurant when I picked up dinner the other night."

"Do you think he knew who you were?"

"He didn't act like it."

Blood leaked from Fried's mouth, but he managed to give them a parody of a smile.

His eyes went to Jamie. "Were you here before?"

"Yes."

"How…?"

"In my nightmares."

"I…knew…something." He closed his eyes. Then they snapped open again. "You haven't won. It's not over…" he gasped before he went still.

Jamie looked at Mack. "What does that mean?"

"I don't know," he answered. "But we'd better get the hell out of here."

Cautiously, he opened the door to the hallway. When he saw nothing there, he picked up a chair and went toward the front door, where he began bashing the chair against the plywood that covered the windows. The plywood was screwed tightly to the wall and held fast.

"Help. Let us out of here. Somebody let us out," Mack shouted.

To Jamie's astonishment, a familiar voice answered.

"Mack?"

"Brady?"

"Yes. We were trying to get in without getting you killed."

"Fried is dead," Mack answered.

"Can you open the front door?"

"I don't think so. I can't open the windows down here either."

He was about to say something else when an explosion rocked the house.

The first one in the basement had been a fake, designed to scare them. This one was real. The whole structure shook, and Mack and Jamie clung together. When the floor stopped vibrating, flames were already shooting up from a heating vent and smoke was pouring into the hallway.

"What happened?" Jamie gasped out.

"He must have had some mechanism set to go off if he didn't return to his command post. Or maybe he had some kind of button in his pocket that triggered the mechanism when his grip relaxed."

The floor beneath their feet had turned hot. Flames were eating their way up the walls.

"What happened?" Brady shouted from outside.

"Explosion in the basement. Fire. We're going upstairs,"

Mack answered. "Call the fire department." Gripping Jamie's hand, he started up the stairs.

She stumbled after him, her mind trying to take in what had happened. Against all odds, they'd killed Fried, but he had still reached out to finish them off.

Smoke rose around them. When Mack stopped moving, Jamie bumped into him.

"Door," he said. "It's locked."

She moaned, then began to cough.

"Take shallow breaths. He must have the key. I've got to go back and get it."

"No! You can't go down there."

"I have to."

"I'm coming with you."

"The hell you are. Stay here."

He turned and dashed down the stairs, but she couldn't let him go alone. And what good would it do anyway? If something happened to him, she was still trapped.

She could hear him coughing as he disappeared into the smoke. When she lost sight of him, she got low to the floor, knowing that the smoke would rise.

Agonizing moments ticked by. Finally she thought she saw him crawling back toward her through the smoke. Before he reached her, he collapsed, his head hitting the floor.

She wanted to cry out. But she didn't dare waste the breath. Crawling forward, she grabbed his arm, pulling him across the floor as flames licked up the walls.

"Mack. You've got to get up, Mack," she begged.

He lifted his head, looking at her, then firmed his lips. She knew he was making a tremendous effort as he pushed himself forward. They both climbed the stairs on hands and knees, the smoke rising with them.

Finally she bumped into the door.

"The key. Where's the key?"

He held out his fist. Opening his fingers, she found the key he was holding. Somehow she fumbled it into the lock and turned. To her vast relief the door opened, and she tumbled through, then turned to help Mack. He tried to crawl forward, but he had obviously come to the end of his resources.

With all her strength, she pulled him, lugging him through the door and slamming it shut behind them, blocking the smoke.

She dragged clean air into her lungs. But they weren't safe yet. The door had stopped the smoke, but it wasn't going to stop the fire.

Mack had pushed himself up and sat with his head against the wall. She let him stay there for a few moments, then tugged at his arm.

"We have to get out of here."

"I know."

"Can you climb out a window?"

"I hope."

She had started across the floor when a figure loomed in front of them, and she screamed.

"It's okay," the man said. "It's Brady Lockwood." He reached out to steady Jamie. "We found a ladder outside and climbed up."

"Thank God."

Mack pushed himself up.

"Are you okay?" Jamie asked him urgently.

"Yeah."

"You just have to climb down," Brady said. He helped them to the window, and when she looked out Jamie wanted to scream with relief.

In the distance she heard a siren.

"Fire department," Brady said.

He helped her across the window sash, and she began climbing down the ladder, holding the rungs in a death grip, looking up to make sure Mack was following. Another man was holding the ladder at the bottom, and she recognized Hunter Kelley.

They made it to the ground, and she saw she was in the front yard of a gray Victorian mansion.

"Washington Street," she wheezed. They were smack in the elegant part of town.

Firemen rushed toward them. "Are you all right?"

"We are now," Mack answered.

"You were in there?"

"Yes. We need to call the police. The man who's been dumping bodies in the mountains is inside. He kidnapped Ms. Shepherd last night. Then me. Tell the cops we're safe."

Jamie wanted to be alone with Mack, but she knew they had breathed in a lot of smoke, and Mack had hit his head. They needed to see a doctor. She also knew the police were going to have some questions about how they'd gotten involved with Fried. As she thought back over everything that had happened, she took her bottom lip between her teeth.

Mack was immediately on the alert. "What's wrong?"

She leaned toward him. "Maybe..." She paused a moment and whispered, "Don't tell them about the dreams. I don't want to get into that."

He nodded. "Yeah. The cops will have the same questions that I did. But how did we get dragged into this?"

A plausible answer leaped into her mind. "The newspaper articles. I was checking on cases involving Craig. I saw Lynn and Jeanette's names."

"Good thinking."

They had no more opportunity for private conversation because paramedics were rushing toward them.

In no time, Jamie found herself on a stretcher. And then EMTs were checking her and Mack out as they rode to the hospital.

She was glad she'd had the chance to talk to Mack at the house, because the police interviewed them separately in the emergency room, asking questions about how they'd ended up in Fried's funhouse. Their stories matched well enough to satisfy the authorities.

Three hours later, she and Mack were finally released by the cops and the medical staff. She thought they'd get to have a private conversation, but she'd forgotten about Hunter and Brady, who were waiting for them, along with Max and Jed.

"You're cleared to go?" Jed asked.

"Yeah," Mack answered. "And the cops are satisfied with our account of what happened with Fried."

"We've pieced it together from your files," Hunter said. "But you need to write it up."

"I will," Mack said. "But I'd like to wait a few days. I'm still too close to being a rat in Fried's maze."

"Nobody else got out of it alive," Brady said.

"The others were alone. Jamie and I worked as a team," Mack answered. "And we surprised the bastard by knocking down one of his walls and using the plywood as a shield."

"To keep acid from falling on us," Jamie added.

The other detective winced.

"Acid?" Jed asked.

"Yeah. I guess that was his desperation move when he saw we were smarter than he thought."

"I can see why you'd like to distance yourself from it," Hunter said.

Jamie looked from him to Brady. "Thank you both for getting us out of the fire. I know you risked your lives to do it."

"I was just holding the ladder," Hunter said.

"Do you want to go to the Randolph Research facility?" Max asked. "It's not too far from here. And you could relax there."

"If it's okay, I'd rather just go back to our hotel," Jamie said.

"Sure. We'll give you a ride back and have Mack's car brought to the lot," Hunter offered.

"Thank you."

"Your purse was in your mother's house," Brady added, holding it out to her.

Jamie felt her chest tighten as she took her bag. "I wasn't thinking about that. How...how did we get checked into the hospital?"

"We took care of it. Your information was at Light Street." Hunter shifted his weight from one foot to the other. "Your mom was worried about you."

Jamie sucked in a sharp breath. "I wasn't thinking about her, either."

"We told her you're fine."

"Thanks so much."

Brady turned to Mack. "I'm afraid anything you didn't bring out with you burned up in the house."

"Better my wallet than me."

Jamie reached for his hand and clasped it tightly. She wanted to hold him in her arms, but not until they were alone. And he must be having similar feelings about wanting privacy.

Max and Jed left to drive back to Baltimore. Brady and Hunter drove Jamie and Mack to the hotel.

They were silent in the back of the car. Silent in the

lobby and silent in the elevator. Jamie used the key card in her purse to let them in. As soon as Mack had closed the hotel door behind them, she thought he would pull her into his arms. Instead, he stood with his hands at his sides and asked, "Are you trying to hide our relationship from our friends?"

She drew in a quick breath. "No. Of course not."

"But you didn't want to go to the Randolph facility with me."

"I...didn't think I could handle it yet."

"Because you still think it's wrong to be with a guy who...was in love with you when you were still married."

"Were you?"

His fists clenched as he gave her a fierce look. "Yes. But I never would have done anything about it while Craig was alive."

"Oh, Mack." She reached for him, clasping her arms around him, holding him tight, pressing her head against his shoulder. It was wonderful to hold him again. Wonderful to know that he belonged to her now. "I love you. So much." She blinked back tears that stung her eyes. "It's hard to say the rest of it, but I'll do it. I was attracted to you for a long time. And I felt guilty about that, even though I never would have—"

"I know."

"But that's why I had so much trouble admitting that it was all right to love you."

"Jamie."

His arms tightened around her, and they clung together.

Her breath hitched. "One more confession. Maybe I fell in love with Craig because I wanted to. I mean, partly because I knew he could take me away from Gaptown. I feel guilty about that, too."

"Don't second-guess yourself."

She nodded, then raised her head, looking him in the eye. "I've got to ask. Do you still think my dreams are weird?"

"No. I know they're part of who you are. And they saved our lives. We never would have gotten out of that funhouse if you hadn't had some idea of what to expect."

He dragged in a breath, then laughed.

"What?"

"You smell like a smokestack. But that gives me an excuse for taking you to the shower and washing you off."

"You think you smell like petunias?"

Smiling, he reached for her hand and led her into the bathroom, where he turned on the water, and they faced each other, each removing their own clothes.

"This stuff needs to go in a plastic bag," she said.

"Or the trash. Later." He adjusted the water, and they stepped into the tub together, reaching for each other. Under the running water, they clung together, swaying in each other's arms. The mood turned quickly from happy to erotic.

Her hands stroked his strong back and shoulders, then his butt and powerful thighs. She touched him everywhere she could reach.

"Thank you," she said in a throaty voice.

"For what?"

"For not giving up on me." For pushing past the barriers that she'd erected between them.

"I couldn't. Even when I didn't know how it was going to come out."

"Thank you," she said again. He ended the conversation

by covering her mouth with his. They clung together under the pounding water, his erection wedged between them.

Reaching behind her, he grabbed the soap, slicked his hands and began running them over her skin, sending tingles over her body.

He handed the bar to her, and she lathered her own hands, sliding them over his skin. Her pulse quickened as she felt the effect on him.

"You are wicked," he muttered.

"I'm trying to be uninhibited."

"Yeah. But we'd better get clean, before we forget what we're supposed to be doing."

They washed quickly and when neither could wait another minute, he braced his back against the wall and lifted her up in his arms. As he held her he entered her, slowly yet commandingly.

Heat infused her with each thrust and she rode him in wild, frantic movements. All too soon he brought both of them to a rocketing climax.

When he eased her feet back to the tub, she leaned against him, her breath coming in hard gasps.

"Thank God I've got you," Mack whispered. "I was scared spitless when he took you."

"I know. I never should have gone out alone."

"He studied you. He knew how to lure you somewhere he could grab you."

She nodded against his shoulder, then sighed as reality invaded.

"What is it?"

"We've got to go back to Mom's and make sure she knows I don't blame her."

"We will. After I get some more quality time with you." He stroked her shoulder and dropped kisses on her face. "You need to know it was Landon who went after you in the parking lot. He said you didn't belong up here, and he was trying to chase you away."

She winced. "He's not real nice. Or real smart. I mean, trying to run me down was a pretty stupid move."

"Well, he was loyal to your mom. When he came in and found her tied up and me standing over her, he thought I'd done it and attacked me."

Jamie gasped. "Oh no. I didn't know about any of that. I can't imagine what you must think of my family. That first visit with Mom was bad enough."

"I told you, mine's not real conventional either." He dragged in a breath and let it out. "We both had it tough as kids. Which is why we're going to make our marriage work."

"Marriage?"

He went still. "I guess I'm getting ahead of myself. Jamie, will you marry me?"

"Yes," she breathed. "Oh yes."

He held her tighter. "I want that. I want to share my life with you."

"Oh yes!"

She leaned up for a kiss and when she could breathe again said, "When we go over to Mom's, don't beat up Landon." She smiled at Mack.

"I won't. He's a creep, but he's not all bad."

"You picked an odd way to find that out."

"Just tell me we don't have to spend the holidays with them."

She laughed. "The holidays? No way. You wouldn't want to eat my mom's burnt gravy. I think we're going to make our own holiday traditions."

"Lots of traditions," he agreed.

She clung to him, so thankful that her life had taken

this turn. Mack Steele had given her a second chance at happiness, and she was going to make the most of every moment they had together.

* * * * *

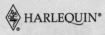 HARLEQUIN®

INTRIGUE®

COMING NEXT MONTH

Available February 8, 2011

#1257 SEIZED BY THE SHEIK
Cowboys Royale
Ann Voss Peterson

#1258 SCENE OF THE CRIME: BACHELOR MOON
Carla Cassidy

#1259 DARKWOOD MANOR
Shivers
Jenna Ryan

#1260 GUNNING FOR TROUBLE
Mystery Men
HelenKay Dimon

#1261 BRAZEN
The McKenna Legacy
Patricia Rosemoor

#1262 .38 CALIBER COVER-UP
Angi Morgan

REQUEST YOUR FREE BOOKS!

2 FREE NOVELS
PLUS 2
FREE GIFTS!

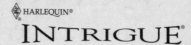

HARLEQUIN®

INTRIGUE®

Breathtaking Romantic Suspense

YES! Please send me 2 FREE Harlequin Intrigue® novels and my 2 FREE gifts (gifts are worth about $10). After receiving them, if I don't wish to receive any more books, I can return the shipping statement marked "cancel." If I don't cancel, I will receive 6 brand-new novels every month and be billed just $4.24 per book in the U.S. or $4.99 per book in Canada. That's a saving of at least 15% off the cover price! It's quite a bargain! Shipping and handling is just 50¢ per book.* I understand that accepting the 2 free books and gifts places me under no obligation to buy anything. I can always return a shipment and cancel at any time. Even if I never buy another book from Harlequin, the two free books and gifts are mine to keep forever.

182/382 HDN E5MG

Name _____ (PLEASE PRINT)

Address _____ Apt. #

City _____ State/Prov. _____ Zip/Postal Code

Signature (if under 18, a parent or guardian must sign)

Mail to the **Harlequin Reader Service:**
IN U.S.A.: P.O. Box 1867, Buffalo, NY 14240-1867
IN CANADA: P.O. Box 609, Fort Erie, Ontario L2A 5X3
Not valid for current subscribers to Harlequin Intrigue books.

**Are you a subscriber to Harlequin Intrigue books and
want to receive the larger-print edition? Call 1-800-873-8635 today!**

* Terms and prices subject to change without notice. Prices do not include applicable taxes. N.Y. residents add applicable sales tax. Canadian residents will be charged applicable provincial taxes and GST. Offer not valid in Quebec. This offer is limited to one order per household. All orders subject to approval. Credit or debit balances in a customer's account(s) may be offset by any other outstanding balance owed by or to the customer. Please allow 4 to 6 weeks for delivery. Offer available while quantities last.

Your Privacy: Harlequin is committed to protecting your privacy. Our Privacy Policy is available online at www.eHarlequin.com or upon request from the Reader Service. From time to time we make our lists of customers available to reputable third parties who may have a product or service of interest to you. If you would prefer we not share your name and address, please check here. ☐

Help us get it right—We strive for accurate, respectful and relevant communications. To clarify or modify your communication preferences, visit us at www.ReaderService.com/consumerschoice.

HI10R

HARLEQUIN®

A Romance

FOR EVERY MOOD™

Spotlight on
Classic

Quintessential, modern love stories
that are romance at its finest.

See the next page
to enjoy a sneak peek from
the Harlequin® Romance series.

*Harlequin Romance author Donna Alward is loved
for her gorgeous rancher heroes.*

*Meet Wyatt as he's confronted by both a precious
little pink bundle left on his doorstep and his neighbor Elli
who's going to show him the ropes....*

Introducing
PROUD RANCHER, PRECIOUS BUNDLE

THE SQUAWKING QUIETED as Elli picked the baby up, and
Wyatt turned around, trying hard to ignore the feelings of
inadequacy as Darcy immediately stopped fussing.

"Maybe she's uncomfortable. What do you think, sweetheart?" Elli turned her conversation to the baby.

"What do you think is wrong?" Wyatt asked, putting the
coffee pot back on the burner.

A strange look passed over Elli's face, one that looked
like guilt and panic. But it was gone quickly. "I couldn't
say," she replied.

"But you were so good with her this afternoon." Wyatt
put his hands on his hips.

"Lucky, that's all. I just…remembered a few things."
The same strange look flitted over her features once more.

Wyatt took the coffee to the table. "You fooled me. You
looked like you knew exactly what you were doing." So
much so that Wyatt had felt completely inept. A feeling he
despised. He was used to being the one in control.

Elli and Darcy walked the length of the kitchen and
back. After a few moments, she admitted, "I haven't really
cared for a baby before. The things I thought of were simply
things I'd heard about. Not from experience, Mr. Black."

Her chin jutted up, closing the subject but making him

want to ask the questions now pulsing through his mind. But then he remembered the old saying—*Don't look a gift horse in the mouth.* He'd benefit from whatever insight she had and be glad of it.

"I don't really know what babies need," he said. "I fed her, patted her back like you did, walked her to sleep, but every time I put her down…"

Wyatt almost groaned. Of course. He'd forgotten one important thing. He'd been so focused on getting the formula the right temperature that he'd forgotten to check her diaper. Not that he had any clue what to do there either.

Pulling calves and shoveling out stalls was far less intimidating than one tiny newborn.

"She's probably due for a diaper change, isn't she." He tried to sound nonchalant. This was a perfect opportunity. Elli must know how to change a diaper. He could simply watch her so he'd know better for the next time.

Instead, Elli came around the corner of the counter and placed Darcy back in his arms. "Here you go, Uncle Wyatt," she said lightly. "You get diaper duty. I'll fix the coffee. Cream and sugar?"

Oh boy, Wyatt thought, looking down into Darcy's pursed face, his smug plan blown to smithereens. He was in for it now.

Will sparks fly between Elli and Wyatt?

Find out in
PROUD RANCHER, PRECIOUS BUNDLE
Available February 2011 from Harlequin Romance

Try these Healthy and Delicious Spring Rolls!

INGREDIENTS

2 packages rice-paper
spring roll wrappers
(20 wrappers)

1 cup grated carrot

¼ cup bean sprouts

1 cucumber, julienned

1 red bell pepper, without
stem and seeds, julienned

4 green onions
finely chopped—
use only the green part

DIRECTIONS

1. Soak one rice-paper wrapper
   in a large bowl of hot water
   until softened.

2. Place a pinch each of carrots,
   sprouts, cucumber, bell
   pepper and green onion on the
   wrapper toward the bottom
   third of the rice paper.

3. Fold ends in and roll tightly
   to enclose filling.

4. Repeat with remaining
   wrappers. Chill before
   serving.

NTRSERIESJAN

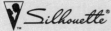

SUSPENSE

Sparked by Danger, Fueled by Passion.

NEW YORK TIMES BESTSELLING AUTHOR

RACHEL LEE

No Ordinary Hero

Strange noises...a woman's mysterious disappearance
and a killer on the loose who's too close for comfort.

With no where else to turn, Delia Carmody looks
to her aloof neighbour to help, only to discover
that Mike Windwalker is no ordinary hero.

CONARD COUNTY *THE NEXT GENERATION*

Available in February.
Wherever books are sold.

Visit Silhouette Books at www.eHarlequin.com

SRS27709R2